Totally Bound Publishing books by Amelia Kingston

So Far, So Good
So, That Got Weird
This is So Happening
So Wrong, it's Wright

I0616576

So Far, So Good

SO WRONG, IT'S WRIGHT

AMELIA KINGSTON

So Wrong, It's Wright
ISBN # 978-1-83943-934-6
©Copyright Amelia Kingston 2020
Cover Art by Erin Dameron-Hill ©Copyright November 2020
Interior text design by Claire Siemaszkiewicz
Totally Bound Publishing

SO WRONG, IT'S WRIGHT

Dedication

To you, my fabulous and amazing readers!
Without you, I'm just a crazy lady in the corner of
the coffee shop making weird faces and talking to
herself.

Chapter One

Michelle

Fuck love. That lying, cheating, no-good emotion can shrivel up and die for all I care. I'm done with the involuntary heart palpitations and suffocating in breathless moments. Done with the hoping and waiting and crying. Done with not being enough.

College is over. This trip, today, is the first day of my new life. A new me. Strong. Independent. And blissfully oh-so-single. I am the master of my own fate and so help me gawd, I *will* be happy.

I grab my Louis Vuitton bag, a graduation gift from my dad, and tumble out of my Mini Cooper. My body is stiff from the long drive and my heart is sore from its long journey.

I stretch out my arms and legs, taking in the unbelievable scenery around me. A city girl, I'd prefer a five-star hotel spa over the dirty wilderness. I'm with Dorothy—lions and tigers and bears are not my deal. But with the rolling mountains, a massive forest and the tranquil blue lake, I can't deny how beautiful it is here. I can take a deep breath for the first time in months.

When Elizabeth said I could stay at her family's summer place for the week, I was too eager for an escape to say no. I know Elizabeth is rich, but when she said *'cabin by the lake'* I pictured a quaint, rustic house. Maybe a small dock with a rowboat. *Nope.*

The two-story lake house in front of me belongs in an architectural magazine. It's beautiful, from its river rock columns and wood siding to its steep fairy-tale roof and many chimneys. Floor-to-ceiling windows make up the entire front, allowing for panoramic views of the majestic crystal-clear lake and tall redwood trees. A wide deck wraps around the first floor, opening up to a path down to the water. Perched on the edge of the lake isn't a dock. It's a full boat house that looks to hold an assortment of watercraft, ranging from canoes to a small yacht.

There's no sign of another human being. No other homes along the lake. No sounds of cars or people, just the gentle hum of crickets. If I weren't boycotting love, I could certainly fall for the magic of this place. It was well worth the six-hour drive, the last two on a private dirt road that was harrowing in the Mini. I'm pretty sure I lost my muffler about halfway up. But I was determined to get away.

I square my shoulders, stand up straight and march into the house. Dumping my suitcase and purse in the entryway, I pinch myself, looking around the beautiful space. The high ceilings and open floorplan make me feel nearly as tiny as the giant forest I just drove through. My entire college apartment could fit inside the living room, but the place still manages to feel homey. Natural colors and soft lighting make it sweetly country without being over-the-top kitschy. Yep. I could get used to this.

I pull out my phone to text Elizabeth, only to remember she said there wouldn't be any cell service. Makes sense. I'm pretty far into the wilderness here. I dig out the paper she gave me and log in to the house's wi-fi, thanking the internet gods that there are ways to communicate without cell service. I snap a few quick pictures of the place and email them to Elizabeth with a handful of emojis and OMGs. My phone chimes with a Facetime notification.

"You made it there safe, I see." Elizabeth's gentle smile lights up my screen.

"You weren't kidding. That drive is no joke. But man, it was worth it. Lizbit, this place is *amazing*." I hold my phone up so she can see the setting sun over the lake behind me. "It's perfect. Thank you so much!"

"Have you seen the bathroom yet?" Elizabeth bites her lip.

"No…"

"Down the hall, third door on the right."

I inch down the hallway with hesitant steps. "I'm not going to find anything freaky in there like an iguana or something?"

"Iguana?"

"My uncle had one when I was little. It lived in the bathtub of his spare bedroom. Scared the crap out of me once. Literally."

Her sweet laugh echoes down the long, empty hall. "No reptiles, I promise."

With a light push, the bathroom door creaks open and I peer into the darkness. I fumble for the light switch on the wall, totally unable to find the stupid thing.

"It's on the far wall," Elizabeth tells me.

I groan. "Why would you put a light switch on the other side of the bathroom?" I grope along the wall until I feel the switch and flick it on, only to be blinded by the sight. I blink a few times before I'm able to take in the majesty in front of me. A huge claw-foot tub, big enough for three of me, sits in the middle of the far wall. A backsplash of river rock gives it a natural feel.

"There's a remote on the wall next to the light switch."

"The bathtub has a remote?"

Elizabeth shakes her head. "Not the bathtub, silly. It controls the entire bathroom," she tells me, as if that somehow makes more sense. "Press the button that looks like a waterfall." Excitement pours out of her.

I click the button, which sure enough looks like a waterfall. The rock wall behind the tub begins to pour water down its face, making a soothing sound that relaxes my whole body.

"Now press the fire button," Elizabeth's giddy voice calls out.

"The fire button? What about earth and air?" I tease, pressing the button as instructed, because, let's be honest, I'm desperate to know what else this magical bathroom's capable of. A panel slides open across from the tub and a fire lights up inside a small crevice.

My mouth drops open. "This. Place. Is. AMAZING!"

Elizabeth laughs at my bewilderment.

"I'm going to have to let you go, Lizbit. I've been consumed with a desperate need to get naked in your bathroom."

"Bath balms are under the sink. Towels are in the closet down the hall. Liquor is in the cabinet next to the bookshelf in the living room and wine's in the cellar. Enjoy yourself, Michelle. You deserve it, babe."

I barely give her time to finish before I hang up and start running myself a bath.

Small amendment to the anti-love policy – inanimate objects, which are physically incapable of betraying me, are now allowed to be loved. Starting with this bathtub.

I settle into the hot soapy water and listen to the sound of rain pouring down as a summer storm breaks outside.

Chapter Two

Drew

My wipers are on full speed and I can still barely see out my windshield. I turned off the main road over an hour ago and I sure as fuck hope I get to Elizabeth's place in the next few minutes or I'm going to end up sleeping in my damn truck. I start up a slight grade and my tires slip in the mud.

I curse myself for the hundredth time for running off on this little adventure like a damn drama queen. It's not really my style. I'm the steady, easygoing one. *Old reliable*, my sisters always tease. As the youngest in the family, I've spent a lifetime getting razzed and learning how to take things in stride.

I don't let myself get riled up easily, but I need a few days to myself right now. A few days to breathe and just *be*. No one asking me how I'm preparing for training camp or how excited I am for my rookie season. Or, my personal favorite, what's the signing bonus for my contract?

I've wanted to play in the NFL since I could carry a football, but I've had my fill of the off-field bullshit. Of everyone thinking they deserve a piece of me. Since I registered for the draft, my life has been consumed with interviews, press conferences and public appearances. And when I went in the first round, *shit*. My private life imploded.

I'm used to questions about the game or my performance, but I wasn't prepared for this craziness. Every aspect of my life is fair game now. What's worse, the people I care about were dragged into this circus too. My teammates. My friends. My family. Everyone is being hounded for the most asinine gossip about me.

What's my favorite pre-game snack? *Who cares?* What do I do in the off-season? *None of your business.* Is there a special woman in my life? *Get fucked.*

Is it so much to ask for everyone to just leave me the hell alone? What I do on the field speaks for itself.

The last straw was a reporter from ESPN surprising my parents on our farm during Christmas break. My mom was horrified. I spent two hours trying to calm her down, listening to her regret the 'scandal' of being filmed in her 'barn clothes'.

No one gets to make my mom feel *less than*, especially not some uninvited pencil-dick reporter. My dad's typical stoic response was spot on — '*It just ain't right.*'

I told my agent this shit has to stop. Her response — '*Feed the beast*' and hiring me a publicist. A fucking *publicist*, like some Hollywood starlet with a drug problem. For the past few months we've been 'cultivating an image', whatever the hell that means.

I'd take three-a-day practices in the dead of summer over all this social media bullshit. I have one skill —

sacking quarterbacks. And that's all I want to keep doing.

Instead I'm posting sweaty post-workout pics on Instagram and tweeting about the ingredients of my protein shake. To my utter surprise, people gobble that shit up. I've got like half a million followers and counting. It's a delicate balance, giving just enough fluff to keep them off my back while keeping as much of my private life *private* as possible.

Jesus, I just want to play football.

When my teammate, Austin, offered up his girlfriend's cabin out in the middle of nowhere, I jumped on it. No cell service, no problem. My country ass is fucking ecstatic at the idea of not seeing or hearing another human being for a few days.

First, I need to make it there without dying in this summer typhoon. It doesn't help that I've got to piss like a racehorse. I didn't realize quite how far it was to the middle of nowhere. If it weren't dropping buckets outside I'd just pull over and answer nature's call, but fuck that.

I look around the floorboards of my truck, wondering how much of a mess I'd make trying to piss into an old two-liter bottle, when the forest falls away and a gigantic house comes into view. *Holy shit.* This place is a damn resort. It's dark as shit and the rain is really coming down, so I can't see much of the detail. But the sheer size of this thing is impressive.

I throw the truck into Park, grab my duffel bag and run up to the porch. I'm a little surprised when I find the front door unlocked and a few lights on. Then again, knowing Austin's girlfriend, she probably asked someone to come out here to prep the place, stock the fridge and shit. She's sweet as hell and too damn good for Austin.

I charge into the house, shaking myself like a golden retriever in the massive entryway. I drop my bag and stomp off to find the nearest toilet. I stare down a long hallway that has about a million doors and grumble. *Definitely going to piss my pants.*

One of the doors about halfway down is cracked and a flickering light has me charging toward it like a moth to a flame. I nudge the door open with my foot. My pants are already unzipped and my dick is in my hand. It's dimly lit, but definitely a bathroom. *Jackpot.*

I skim my hand over the wall but can't find a light switch. I'm scanning the room looking for the toilet when a bloodcurdling scream makes me drop my dick and jump about three feet in the air — pretty impressive for a guy who's six-foot-three. The acrobatics have my pants sliding off my ass. I shuffle around in the dim light, pants around my ankles, dick out and my bladder completely forgotten. My heart is pounding. My gaze snaps to the bathtub and the source of the feminine screams.

A petite woman bolts upright in the tub, sloshing water over the sides. The only light in the room is a fire to her side and it casts a warm glow over her body. Her very naked, very *wet* body. I can see every inch of her from the tip of her head to her cute belly button. A patch of bubbles slides down her shoulder, gliding across her sharp collarbone before sinking between her perky round tits. I'd love to trace the same path with my tongue. It's only been a few heartbeats, but I'm frozen in time, devouring every inch of her glistening skin.

"Fuck me," I stutter on a labored breath.

She wraps an arm around her chest and my gaze finally makes it up to her face. She's not scared — she's furious.

She points behind me and shouts, "Get the hell out of here, Andrew Wright!"

I shake my head at the sound of my own name. I've got to be dreaming. Maybe I flipped my truck back on that dirt road out in the rain and this is all some crazy coma-induced hallucination.

"Now!" she screeches while I stare at her soft, round face in wonder.

Pert upturned nose, flushed cheeks, full heart-shaped lips, deep brown eyes and long silky black hair that begs to be coiled in my fist. My brain kicks back into gear and anger takes the place of lust. *Michelle Anders.* My eyes narrow on her, my jaw tightens and I scowl.

I glance at the toilet next to her and take a step toward it.

"Don't you dare," she chides.

I lift the lid without a word.

"You wouldn't."

I grab my dick and she slaps her hands over her face. "Oh my God! You're an animal."

I'm sporting a semi, so it takes a few seconds to get going, but I'm determined to do my business, naked prissy girl in the bathtub be damned.

I leave the seat up, zip and strut to the sink to wash my hands.

"You are so disgusting."

"Chill out. I'm washing my hands."

"Close the door behind you."

I don't.

I stalk back out to the living room and pull out my phone. I try to call Austin, but it doesn't go through. Right, no cell service. I toss my phone onto the coffee table, fall into the couch, slouch back against the cushions and stare up at the ceiling. Of all the people in

16

the world, it had to be her? The rain is beating down hard and I focus on the sound, instead of the image of Michelle's soap-covered naked body.

Chapter Three

Michelle

Now that I know I'm not going to be murdered in the world's most luxurious bathroom, I'm absolutely livid. Goddamn Drew and his smug, crass ass. Just when I was starting to think things were going my way, in stumbles the country-boy jock who pulverized the last bit of my heart.

Is there no justice in the world?

Clearly not, because if so, Drew would shrivel up into a broken nothingness. But he hasn't. No, instead he looks healthy, strong and sexy as hell. Even soaking wet with his pants around his ankles, he's delicious. Maybe *especially* soaking wet. I clamp my eyes tight, willing away the sight of Drew's penis.

My bath is officially ruined. I flick on the lights and turn off the fire and water fountain with an unsatisfied huff. I dry off with a towel that's been woven out of fluffy clouds, but it does nothing to soothe my anger.

I didn't bring my bag into the bathroom, so now I get to throw my dirty clothes back on. I'm seething when I message Elizabeth.

Drew is here!!!

Who? Drew Wright?

No. Drew Barrymore. Yes, Drew Wright!

Why?

I have no freaking idea!!! Maybe you could tell me.

Three little dots appear and disappear about a dozen times. I'm fully dressed, but still hiding in the bathroom. The rest of the house is quiet and for a moment I wonder if I hallucinated it all.

I snatch my phone off the counter and crack the door. Peeking out, I look for the mountain of a man who was born to torture me. I pad out to the living room and freeze when I spot his shaggy brown hair dangling off the back of the couch. His arms are thrown over his face and he looks exhausted. I could almost feel bad for him if I didn't know what a colossal jerk he really is. My phone chimes in my hand and I yelp. Drew sits up and turns to look at me.

I snap my shoulders back and straighten up. I answer Facetime quickly with, "Hello?" like I don't know it's Elizabeth.

"Okay, so obviously there's been a little mix-up."

"Go on," I say, my eyes focused on the ceiling to avoid Drew's heated gaze on me.

"Austin told me Drew would be using the cabin the last week of June. Which clearly I thought meant the actual last week, not the last *full* week of June."

"You mean the first week of July?" Austin chimes in from over Elizabeth's shoulder.

Drew shoves off the couch and rounds the corner until he's standing ten feet in front of me. He interlocks his fingers behind his head, making his already massive body seem to take up half of the gigantic living space. He's solid like a tank, a foot taller than me and probably a foot wider too. The corners of his soft lips drop to a pout and his warm honey-brown eyes I used to get lost in burn a hole straight through me. His shoulders are tense and his biceps flex. I swallow hard. *At least his pants are zipped.*

"I'm sorry, guys," Elizabeth apologizes, gnawing on her lip.

Austin snags the phone out of her hand and his pretty-boy face takes up the whole screen. "It's not that big of a deal. You guys can share, right?" he teases.

"You can't be serious?" Drew asks, glaring at me like this is all my fault.

"That's not going to work for me," I snap.

Drew drops his arms, tucks his hands into his pockets and slouches forward. "Me neither."

"Oh, come on. The place is huge—you guys wouldn't even have to see each other unless you wanted to."

"I've seen all there is to see of the little princess here." He shrugs. "I'm good."

My lips pucker like I'm sucking on a lemon. "You're disgusting."

He chuckles, a dry and sarcastic sound that doesn't suit him. "You've mentioned that already."

I stand as tall as I can, lifting on to my tiptoes for that extra quarter inch, and stare up at Drew as I tell Austin, "Please explain to your brute of a friend that I was here first and if he were any kind of gentleman at all, he'd leave."

"Look, I—"

Drew cuts off his friend and takes a step toward me. "Austin, could you tell this spoiled brat that gentleman or not, no one in their right mind would go out on that death trap of a road in the middle of a damn thunderstorm?

Mother nature must be on his side, because a flash of lightning across the lake shines in through the windows, followed quickly by the loud rumble of thunder.

Undaunted by Drew or mother nature, I take a step closer, meeting his challenge. "Could you tell him that a real man wouldn't be scared of a little rain?"

Drew steps forward again, the space between us shrinking by the second. "Can you tell her that a real man doesn't get scared off by a midget harpy?"

Facetime forgotten, my hand drops, my mouth falls open and I suck in a sharp breath. "I'd rather be a midget harpy than an overgrown Neanderthal."

He takes another step toward me and crosses his arms. He's so close now I have to crane my neck to meet his eyes, but I'll be damned if I'm going to be the one that loses this staring contest.

"At least this overgrown Neanderthal knows how to lock a bathroom door." He quirks an eyebrow and drops his gaze to my chest. I instinctively cross my arms over my breasts even though I'm now fully dressed.

I lurch forward, shoving my crossed arms into his solar plexus. He doesn't budge. Why would he? He could bench press me if he wanted to. I am furious. At him. At the situation. At the fact that he can make me feel so insignificant. "I should slap that smirk off your stupid face," I growl, my blood boiling.

He leans down, his face in mine when he chides, "Try it, princess."

"Time out. Time. OUT!" Elizabeth screeches. "There will be no bloodshed in my family's lake house!"

"Pity," I scoff with a snarl. I spin away, satisfaction washing over me at the sound of my still-wet hair slapping across his face. I retreat to the other side of the living room, trying desperately to slow my heart rate before I do something I'm going to regret.

"It's obviously too late and too stormy for anyone to go anywhere tonight." Elizabeth tries to reason with both of us. I let out a deep sigh, accepting the truth when it's presented by my friend instead of my nemesis. "In the morning, we'll figure out who stays and if someone has to go."

"*Who* has to go," I correct.

"We'll flip a coin," Drew adds.

"Fine."

"In the meantime..." Austin's voice rings out of my speakers again. "May I suggest you guys get wasted and *try* to make nice?"

Chapter Four

Drew

Michelle ends the video chat and I realize I'm trapped here with her for the night. I'm opening up every cabinet in the kitchen, looking for the booze.

"He wasn't serious," Michelle calls to my back.

I blow out a raspberry. "He sure as fuck was. Do you even know Austin?"

"You're probably right. All you football players are the same. Big, drunk, cheating assholes."

I slam a cabinet closed and chide myself for it. *Chill out.* I spin around and pin her with a death stare. "We are *not* all the same. Just because you picked the biggest piece of shit to ever put on a jersey doesn't mean the rest of us are."

"You're about as loyal as a toad."

"You wouldn't know loyalty if it bit you in your uptight ass."

She doesn't answer. Instead, she stalks into the living room and pulls open a cabinet door, revealing just about every type of liquor you could ever want. "Here, before you tear down the house."

"Thank fuck." I stalk over to the bar. My arm brushes against her shoulder, but she doesn't flinch. I'm sure she hates touching me, but she's a stubborn little thing.

I'd swear she counts to ten in her head before pulling away. Without a word, she rolls her brand-new, expensive-as-hell-looking bag down the hallway. I watch her walk away, eyeing the soft curve of her hips and wondering what the rest of her would look like wet and soapy. Princess is a real piece of work, but I would hate-fuck the shit out of that woman.

I pour myself three fingers of whiskey and take a long sip. It's going to be a hell of a night.

The cabin is cold, but I'm toasty after polishing off my second glass of whiskey. Still, the sounds of thunder and rain are rolling over us and that giant fireplace is calling to me, begging for a roaring fire. It's not like I've got anything better to do, with no TV and no cell service. I could ask Michelle for the wi-fi password, but that would require talking to her and I'd rather set myself on fire.

There's a few massive logs next to the hearth. I think they're mostly for show, but they're dry and should burn fine. I look around for something to split them with, but come up empty. I step outside and do a lap of the wrap-around porch. At the back of the house there's a small shed with a larger wood pile against one wall. There's got to be something in that shed that will work. Too bad it's going to take a fifty-yard dash across the yard to get there.

I sprint across the lawn, dodging the larger puddles, but still end up soaked when I make it to the shed. I pull the latch, glad that it's not locked. I flip the switch on the wall and an overhead light fills the small space. I love the smell of wood, rust and rain. It reminds me of home. I close my eyes and take a long, deep breath, bathing in the memories of the farm I grew up on. The loud rumble of thunder outside reminds me an old shed isn't the ideal place to spend my night. I grab a large hatchet off a hook on the wall and make my way back to the house.

My clothes are dripping by the time I make it inside, so I strip them off, tossing them onto the large stone hearth. I strut to the bar in my boxer briefs and pour myself another whiskey. Now, time to get this fire started.

Chapter Five

Michelle

I'm so mad I could scream, but I wouldn't dare give Drew the satisfaction. I'm furious at Drew, and Elizabeth, and Austin, and the rain. And this entire stupid situation I'm stuck in. As idiotic as Austin's suggestion is — that Drew and I *both* spend the week locked in this remote lake house — that idea about getting drunk isn't half bad. Not that I'd ever admit it, but I could use something to take the edge off. Drew drives me up the damn wall. He's big. And loud. And *primal*.

I sneak down to the cellar and grab a bottle of wine, snagging a wine key and glass off the shelf before slipping back into my room. I change into my most comfortable pajamas, a pink tank top and my short-shorts with cats riding unicorns — a Christmas present from Elizabeth.

I pour myself a big girl glass of wine, to the brim, grab my tablet and climb into bed. Getting cozy, I open up the sports romance I downloaded on my way here. It's a new release from one of my favorite authors that I've been desperate to dive into. I may have sworn off jocks in real life, but they're still my favorite book boyfriends.

I'm five Chapters and three glasses of wine in when I have to stop. It's hot. *Very* hot, full of enemies-to-lovers angst and sexual tension. Unfortunately, Drew ruins it, like he ruins everything. Knowing we're alone out here in the woods, that he's in the next room, keeps my mind drifting back to him. To that hungry look in his eyes when he watched me in the tub. Instead of the egotistical hero, I picture Drew with all his ripped muscles and rough words. Instead of the sassy heroine, I picture myself, teasing and torturing him until he can't stand it. Until he pins me down and destroys me.

Urgh.

I toss my tablet aside with a frustrated sigh. I refuse to get all hot and bothered thinking about that brute. I loathe him. I don't care if he is the perfect hate-fuck fantasy. There is no way in hell I want his hard body pressing me into the mattress, trapping my arms above my head, my teeth digging into his shoulder while he tears me apart with that massive—

Stop it!

I jump off the bed and give myself a light slap on each cheek. *Snap out of it.* I take a deep breath, count to ten and pour myself another tall glass of wine. When I crawl back into bed, I pull open a suspense novel instead. Murder and mayhem. That sounds a lot safer.

The decapitated body of the mayor's unruly son was just discovered on the steps of city hall when a loud

TWACK has me jumping out of my skin. I stare at my bedroom door, expecting the murderer to kick it down any second. A stark silence fills my bedroom, punctuated by my thudding heart.

TWACK. Silence. *TWACK.* Silence. *TWACK.*
What the hell?

My alcohol-soaked brain is racing with possibilities for the loud and violent sound. Eventually, my curiosity outweighs my sense of self-preservation and I have to know what that noise is. I toss back the covers and grab my wineglass. Not a weapon. Not my cell phone. My wineglass. A girl's gotta have priorities.

I crack my door, expecting to see Freddie or Jason charging toward me, but the hallway is empty. I head toward the sound, kicking myself for being like every stupid woman in every slasher flick. I shake the thought out of my head. I'm perfectly safe. This isn't a horror movie. Besides, someone would have to get past Drew first. He hates me, but not enough to let an ax murderer get at me. *I don't think.*

I tiptoe into the living room, quiet as a mouse. The rhythmic hacking has stopped and the stark silence is somehow creepier. I peek around the corner and don't see anyone in the large living room or foyer. I pinch my eyebrows together and tilt my head. *Did I imagine it?*

The seeming emptiness — and maybe the alcohol — makes me idiotically brave. I charge into the living room, but come to a screeching halt when I see Drew rise from where he was hunched over in front of the fireplace. He pushes himself up to his full height and I'm dumbstruck. He is in nothing but a pair of tight boxer briefs that are slightly askew and hanging low on his hips. They look painted on his deliciously thick thighs. His firm ass is pure perfection with two sexy dimples, just above the hem of his boxers, begging to be licked. His back glistens with a light sweat and I picture raking my nails across his skin.

"Fuck me," I murmur.

At the sound of my desperate, breathy voice, Drew turns and I about faint. I've never seen anything so sexy. I drink him in, long eyelashes to thick calves. His shaggy brown hair hangs over his gentle eyes, making him look adorably nefarious. He slings an ax over his shoulder and his abs ripple in the firelight. The chiseled V dipping into his boxers draws my attention down to the impressive bulge that has my mouth watering. He is powerful and dangerous. The wild mountain man is my new favorite fantasy.

Our eyes lock and I swear every muscle in my body goes limp. That's the only explanation for my mouth dropping open and my wineglass slipping out of my hand. It shatters into a thousand pieces on the tile floor and the wine splashing on my feet snaps me out of my stupor.

I stare down at the shards, but lack any ability to process the sight. Drew is around the couch in a blink, stepping up beside me close enough that I can smell his woodsy scent.

"Hope that wasn't expensive," he snips and I remember I hate the sexy brute.

Needing space to breathe, I shove him away. *Hard.* "It's your fault. You scared the shit out of me."

"What did I do?"

I gesture to his naked body and the ax he left back by the fireplace. "I thought I was going to be murdered in my sleep! What the hell are you doing?"

"Making a fire," he replies flatly, like I'm the crazy one. Like naked lumberjacking is a thing. *Holy crap, I wish it was a thing.*

I take a step away from him, but his massive hands on my slender shoulders hold me back.

"Watch your step," he placates me.

I slap his hands away. "Don't touch me. And don't tell me what to do. I'm not a child."

"There's broken glass." He points to the shattered remains of my wineglass, about an inch from my bare feet.

"I can see that, and it's your fault." I poke a finger into his hard pec and we both drop our gazes to the simple touch. His face is placid, but his heart is racing with mine. Biting my lip at the warmth spreading across my skin, I slip toward him. He grips my shoulders again, but I remember myself and bat them away.

"Jesus," Drew mumbles as he bends forward and shoves a shoulder into my stomach. Air shoots out of my lungs and the living room turns upside down and spins.

"Put me the hell *down*!" I shriek, pounding on his firm back with that perfect ass staring back at me. I resist the urge to sink my teeth into it.

"You got it, princess," he tells me with a slap to my bare thighs.

He stomps over to the fireplace and starts to set me down on the fluffy rug. Indignant, I squirm and slip out of his hands. All the blood has rushed to my head and I'm not steady on my feet. He moves to catch me, but loses his balance in the process. I grab for him as I topple over, somehow managing to take him with me.

We collapse in a heap on the rug, his body on top of mine, pressing into me and making me tremble.

"Get off me, you brute." My voice is ice cold despite the fire surging through my body and the heat pooling between my thighs. I pound my tiny fists on his broad shoulders with zero effect.

He grabs my wrists and pins them above my head. I shove down the desire to wrap my legs around his hip and pull him into me. Instead, I twist and wriggle, anything to try to escape the titillating weight of his hard body on mine.

"As soon as you calm the fuck down, I will," he coos in my ear.

"You're disgusting," I snip.

He has the nerve to laugh. "Disgusting, huh? Is that why you couldn't take your eyes off me?" His hot breath tickles the delicate skin on my neck. He smells like cedar, expensive whiskey and sweat. "We both know you're a little liar. Careful, princess. Where I come from, liars get punished." He nips at my exposed collarbone and I dig my teeth into my bottom lip to hold back a moan.

"I hate you." I struggle under him, desperate for space. For air. For my sanity.

He shifts his weight and settles between my thighs. His boxers barely restrain his hard length. He presses into me and my eyes roll back in my head. "Hate me or not, you still want to *fuck* me."

"Screw you," is all I can think to say, my mind drowning in wine and desire.

He chuckles. "Like I said…"

I stare up at him, meeting his challenge. I'm desperate not to give away how badly I want him inside me.

"Tell me I'm wrong," he taunts. He grinds against me, the sensation driving me to the edge of madness.

I let out a pathetic whimper when his hard cock hits the apex of my thighs. Still, I have enough self-preservation to say, "You're wrong."

"Little liar." His low voice is husky with want.

He holds both my wrists in one callused hand and I squirm beneath him. Reveling in the contact, I have no desire to get away, but I sure as hell don't want him to think I'm giving in. He runs his free hand down my side. Bunching up the hem of my shirt, he teases the sensitive skin on my stomach with his deft fingers. With his hand and his mouth, he burns a tortuous trail up to my chest. I'm nearly exposed when he brushes the underside of my breast and I arch into him.

"Tell me to stop," he dares.

I refuse to be the one to back down. I stay silent, pressing my mouth into a hard line, cocking an eyebrow and leering up at him. He holds my gaze and an evil smile curls his lips.

The flood gates open and we are consumed by wanton sexual fury.

He rips my shirt off over my head in a single tug, the fabric tangling at my wrists and forming a soft binding. I gasp when his mouth engulfs my hard nipple. I lock my legs around his waist and pull his hips against me. He moans, sliding his wet mouth to my other nipple while he twists and pinches the abandoned one.

He releases my hands and I wrap them around his strong shoulders, raking my nails across his skin as I glide my hands down and grab his ass. I lift my hips as I pull him against me.

"Fuck," he mutters, heady and out of control.

Chapter Six

Drew

"Fuck." My voice is so choked with need I hardly recognize it. Michelle's perfect tits are in my mouth, her hot body's writhing under mine and I'm about to fucking lose it. I want to destroy this woman. She's too fucking stubborn to admit it, but she wants it too.

I'll have her begging soon enough.

I'm not gentle. I'm not sweet. That's not what she wants. The lying little princess likes it rough. She wants to be conquered. She meets me challenge for challenge, and it's sexy as fuck.

I dive between those milky thighs and rip off the pathetic excuse for shorts she's strutting around in. Her knees fall open in a silent welcome. *And she wants to pretend like she's not desperate for this?*

I bite the inside of her thigh hard enough to leave a mark and slide a finger inside her. She's wet. Soaked, but tight as hell. Watching the pleasure on her beautiful face, I reach down into my boxers and stroke myself in the same rhythm I finger her tight pussy.

I'm desperate to be inside her. For release.

Not yet.

I need to hear her lose it first. I want her to know how I can make her feel. How I can own her body. I want her to know what she walked away from.

Before the night is over, this spoiled little princess is going to be screaming my name, begging to take every inch of me.

This is her punishment and my reward. For all the shit she's put me through, I deserve this. I deserve to get off then toss her aside. That's what she did to me.

I shove a second finger inside her and watch as her head falls back and she arches off the rug. She wraps her slender fingers around those soft tits, twisting her nipples and keeping them hard. The sight makes my cock swell. She knows she deserves to be tortured.

I give her a long, slow lick up her soft folds as I drag my fingers out of her. I pull away and stop touching her. I wait.

She lets out a desperate whimper that brings a smile to my lips. I thrust back into her and savagely flick her clit with my tongue. She loves the firm pressure, meeting me with every hard stroke. She's over the edge in minutes, clenching around my fingers harder than I ever imagined her tiny body could.

She's a panting puddle underneath me. I'm still pumping my fingers into her, milking every ounce of pleasure I can out of that tight pussy. I look up at her flushed body and smile, victorious.

There's no denying it now. She's as naughty as they come.

"You like it dirty, don't you, princess?" I chide.

She pops up and pierces me with those dark eyes.

"Shut up and fuck me." Her voice is cold and raspy, her command carrying the edge of desperation. I just about come from her words alone.

I grab the condom out of my wallet in my still-wet pants on the fireplace and roll it on faster than I thought possible. I flip her over on her stomach and prop her up on her knees before she can say a word. This is how I want her, at my mercy.

I grab her small hips and line up with that sweet center. Normally I'd go slow, worried about hurting a girl her size. But not Michelle. She can take every punishing inch. I thrust into her in a single, unforgiving stroke. She gasps as she stretches around my length.

"You're tight. So goddamn tight," I tell her. I stay buried balls-deep inside her, my head falling back with the intense pleasure.

She starts slow, pulling forward before slamming back onto me, fucking herself with my cock.

"You like that cock, princess?" I ask her, eager to hear her admit it.

She doesn't. Instead she lets out a deep moan and tightens around my shaft. I grip her hips and take back control. I set a brutal pace, drilling into her. She takes it with pleasure, gripping the rug and moaning.

"I'm gonna come again," she tells me, and it's the sweetest confession.

I slacken my pace, holding off. "Say my name, princess."

She stays silent and I stop thrusting entirely, seated fully inside her but refusing to move. She tries to pull forward and push back onto me, using my cock to get herself off, but I hold her in place.

"Say my name," I command with a slap to her ass.

She jumps forward with a gasp and my cock slips out of her. She settles back against me, circling her hips with a desperate whimper, but she still doesn't answer. I slap her other cheek, hard.

"Brute," she taunts.

Good enough.

I bury myself inside, fucking her hard and deep. Punishing us both. She comes on my cock, that sweet pussy clenching down on me and wringing out every bit of pleasure until I nearly pass out.

She collapses underneath me and I fall forward, catching myself before I crush her tiny body. Rolling to my side, I lie with one arm draped over her lower back as we catch our breath. I'm not sure I can move. I don't think I want to.

The sound of the storm overhead, the fire crackling and Michelle's satisfied hums beside me settle my mind. With a lazy motion, I pull her body against mine. She curls into me and satisfied exhaustion lulls me into a dead sleep.

When I wake up in the morning, the rain has stopped, the fire is out and Michelle is gone.

Chapter Seven

Michelle

Shit. Shit. Shit. FUUUUCK!

As the afterglow of the best orgasm — best *two* orgasms — of my life fades, realization hits me full force, followed immediately by utter confusion and complete panic. Drew is passed out, a peaceful quasi-smile on his pouty lips. He doesn't even stir when I slip away, grabbing my discarded clothes and scurrying back to my room.

What did I do?

I had *sex* with Andrew Wright.

It's wrong. So very, very wrong. But holy hell did it feel so damn *right*. He was rough and demanding. He owned every inch of my body and demanded my pleasure. It was everything I've always wanted and never dared breathe out loud. I hate being petite. Men are always so careful with me, like I'm fragile. But not

Drew. He fucked me like he was conquering me. And I loved every second of it.

I skirt the broken glass without bothering to clean it up—I've got bigger problems to solve than spilled wine, like what the hell this means and what on earth am I supposed to do now?

I close my door and triple check that it's locked. I pace the bedroom, my head swirling with the past hour of debauchery. I've never had sex like that, dirty and aggressive. I'm the good girl. I've never even slept with a guy I wasn't officially dating before, and now I'm having raunchy sex with a guy I hate on someone else's living room floor?

The wine. It must've been the wine. I snatch the remainder of the bottle off my nightstand and pour it down the sink in the en suite bathroom. I check the ingredients on the label for roofies or ecstasy, something that would explain my complete lack of willpower and discretion. *Nope. Just wine.* I'm a complete idiot.

I turn on the shower and stand under the hot water, trying to burn off the memory of Drew's touch. It doesn't work. I climb out once the water runs cold and my fingers are prune-y. I put on another, much more conservative, pair of pajamas and crawl back into bed. I flick off the light and try to sleep. Instead, I stare up at the ceiling for the rest of the night, images of Drew's body dancing in my mind.

I'm dead tired when the sun starts to pour into my room, but I've finally figured out how to handle it. And by *it*, I mean the wildly inappropriate and devastatingly amazing sex with my mortal enemy. I will take back control of the situation. It happened, but it's over.

It changes nothing. He is still a cold-hearted jerk. And he is definitely still leaving.

My entire body tenses when I hear a light rustling from the living room. I listen intensely to the sound of cabinets closing, dishes clanking and a door slamming shut. When the house goes quiet again, I hop out of bed and get dressed, putting on a long-sleeved T-shirt and long pants, covering every inch of skin I can despite the warm summer weather.

I storm out of my bedroom and into the kitchen with my shoulders back and my head high. I will not show any sign of weakness. I get the coffee pot brewing before turning around to realize Drew isn't even here. I deflate, my false bravado easing out of me.

Standing in the kitchen I can see the entire living room, dining room and foyer area. I take in the space and realize he cleaned up the wine I spilled last night. The place looks pristine, no sign of our encounter at all. I look over at the fluffy rug in front of the long-extinguished fire and my cheeks burn. I avert my eyes and count to ten in my head. When I open them again, I notice a duffel bag still sitting by the front door. It must be Drew's. I lean over to look out of the window, and sure enough, an old pick-up truck is parked on the other side of the huge driveway from my Mini.

I pour myself a cup of coffee and sit at the table to think. Drew is off somewhere, but he'll be back at some point. I plan my confrontational declaration carefully, full of lots of strong words and power stances. I may be small, but my mom taught me how to be intimidating despite my stature. That tiny woman could send Mike Tyson running.

When Drew comes in through the front door twenty minutes later, I'm the picture of inner peace, my legs crossed and shoulders back as I take a slow sip of coffee. He has no idea that my heart is beating against my ribcage and I've been a nervous wreck sitting here waiting for him. Nor does he know that the sight of him back from a run, sweaty and flushed, makes my mouth water. *Guess it wasn't* just *the wine.*

I force my eyes up to his, waiting for him to approach me. He doesn't. He doesn't even look at me. He stalks past me down the hallway like I don't even exist. Like I don't even matter. The shower turns on and I sit there dumbfounded.

I get up, debating going back to my room, but that feels like hiding. I sit back down, but that feels like I'm waiting for him. Which I am, but I can't let it seem that obvious. I go to stand in the kitchen and fidget with the fancy appliances on the counter. I don't turn to look when I hear his bedroom door open. I don't look up when I catch his massive body entering the kitchen in my peripheral vision. I'm cool as can be, flipping through a smoothie recipe book that came with the Vitamix blender.

Without a single acknowledgment, Drew grabs a bowl, spoon, cereal and milk. He skirts around me, avoiding physical contact in a lowkey way, like I'm just another piece of furniture.

He takes his breakfast to the dining room table and has a seat. I've had enough.

Tossing aside my recipe book, I whip around, lock my eyes on him and declare, "You're leaving today."

"Yep," he answers like I was asking a question. His gaze is focused out the massive windows.

I wasn't ready for him to capitulate that fast. I had a whole thing planned. "I...well...good," I stammer. "I was here first. Plus, this is Elizabeth's place, not Austin's, and she's my friend."

He doesn't answer. He's staring at the sun dancing across the lake, his shoulders are relaxed and his focus is clear. Sure, the lake is pretty, but it's not *that* pretty. He's ignoring me and it's aggravating.

"And what happened last night..." I swallow hard. He doesn't look at me, but his loud chewing stops. "Was obviously an impulsive lapse in judgment. Temporary insanity induced by cabin fever. It will *never* happen again."

He drags his eyes up to me, a lecherous grin on his lips when he answers, "Sure it won't, princess."

I puff out my chest and stand up tall. "My name is Michelle, you brute." I meant it as an insult, but my cheeks burn and my legs shake at the memory of calling him that last night. While he was *inside* me. He gives me a knowing smirk before turning back to his cereal.

His spoon drops into his bowl and he pushes back from the table. My eyes follow his movements like a predator. He rounds the kitchen island and drops his dishes in the sink. He's in my space, but I refuse to step away. To back down.

"I know your name. Maybe I'll use it next time, when you're screaming mine." His voice is hard and sultry. My skin prickles at the memories of his demanding touch. He steps away, the smell of soap and aggression going with him. He sweeps his bag off the floor and stalks toward the door. Over his shoulder he tosses, "It's been real...princess."

Chapter Eight

Drew

I toss my bag into the cab of my truck and stare up at the impressive house in front of me, rage seeping out of my every pore. I don't know how such a tiny woman can be such a gigantic pain in the ass. I grip the steering wheel, tightening and twisting my hands around it like it's her scrawny neck.

Sex doesn't always have to mean something. But sex like *that*? I've never felt that crazy, aggressive, all-consuming need to own a woman before. I hate her, but I'm man enough to admit our chemistry is off the charts. A violent passion neither of us can control. There's something real here and she knows it.

Pulling that disappearing act on me was bad enough, but then this morning pretending like last night didn't even happen? That made me feel like nothing. Less than nothing. To her, I'm just another casual fuck. She may be used to it, but I sure as hell am not.

Why is she like this? She can be sweet. I've seen it. The first night we met, she was a sweet little bundle of energy. Giggling and playful in my lap. I believed her when she said she liked me. I trusted it when she kissed me.

That's ancient history now, a manipulative fucking act. Last night was a good reminder that she is not sweet. She's a social-climbing succubus. A fucking cold-blooded viper and I'm lucky she never got her fangs in me.

I should never have touched her. Good as it felt, she doesn't deserve a minute of my time. Not after the shit she pulled. Not after using me to get back at one of my teammates.

I floor it out of the driveway, happy to leave Michelle Anders in my rearview mirror where she belongs.

I roll down my window and breathe in the smell of new rain in an old forest. I focus on the drive, the road even worse now that it's mostly mud. The third time my wheels slide and I lose traction, I shift into four-wheel drive.

My mind flashes back to Michelle's Mini in the driveway this morning. I didn't see it last night in the pouring rain, but it suits her. Petite and perky. She'll never make it up this road in that car. Would she even know what to do if she got stuck? I shake the worry out of my head.

Not my girl. Not my problem.

Around a curve in the road I come to a screeching halt. I barely manage to skid to a stop before crashing into a massive downed tree blocking the way.

"Fuck," I curse and slam my palm on the steering wheel. I let out a long yell into the empty cab before a dry laugh surges out of me. I drop my head back against the seat. "You've got to be kidding me."

* * * *

"Honey, I'm home," I announce, tossing my bag on the foyer's hardwood floor with a *thud*. I stand there waiting for the ass-chewing I'm sure the little brat is going to administer after seeing me back here.

She pops out of her room and takes me in. Her mouth drops open and her eyes blink rapidly in surprise. Her petite body lacks its usual hard stance. Her shoulders are slouched forward and her head lolls to the side. She looks...relieved? That can't be it.

She ambles up to me, those soft brown eyes wide in disbelief. Her advance stills a few feet away, intentionally out of arm's reach.

"What are you doing here?" she asks, more quizzical than hostile.

I unfold my arms, my defenses dropping as I study her round face. Her eyes are puffy and her cheeks are a blotchy red. Without thinking, I step forward and reach out to stroke her face.

"Were you crying?"

She lurches away from me and sucks in a breath. "Tears of joy, brute."

Ah, there she is, my angry little brat.

"Whatever you say, princess." I snatch my bag off the floor, brush past her and head down the hallway to one of the bedrooms.

The pitter-patter of her feet lets me know she's following me.

"I thought you were leaving," she prods, her voice back to the same harsh tone from this morning.

I sit down on the bed and watch her hover in my doorway out of the corner of my eye. I untie my mud-coated shoes and answer, "Storm knocked a tree down. It's blocking the road. Neither of us is going anywhere until someone comes to remove it."

She crosses her arms. "You're such a liar. It wasn't that bad of a storm."

I shake my head. "Don't believe me, then feel free to traipse out there yourself."

"Well, I'm not spending the week locked in here with you," she scoffs.

I stand up and face her. "You know where the door is." I flick open the button of my jeans. "Now, if you don't mind, I'd like to get out of these *filthy* clothes."

"You're such a…"

"Brute? Yeah, I've heard."

She drops her eyes to my fly and darts her pink tongue out to lick her top lip. *Fuck me.* She may be a viper, but my cock's got it bad for this woman.

After a beat, she shakes her head and clears her throat. Blowing out a haughty breath, she quips, "Fine. If you're too scared of a little mud, then I'll leave."

She spins away and stalks off to her room. The house is filled with the frenzied sound of her tossing things back into her suitcase, followed by the stomping of tiny feet across the living room. She slams the front door behind her and I take a deep breath.

I put my hands on my hips and try to talk myself out of going after her. I can either go stop her now or go save her later. I step back into my boots, not bothering to tie them before chasing after her.

She's shoving her suitcase into her back seat and slamming the door shut. I catch the driver's door before she can slam it in my face.

"You'll never make it back in this toy car."

Her eyes narrow and her lips purse. "What do you care?"

"I care not to have to come save your stubborn ass when you get stuck."

"Let's not pretend you're a gentleman. I will be fine."

I grumble and debate letting her go on her merry way. "No. You won't."

"Let. Go. Of. My. Door," she tells me in a clear warning.

"No."

She starts her car and raises an eyebrow. "Suit yourself." She starts to back up and I jump away to avoid getting run over.

"You're crazy, woman."

"Just determined."

Chapter Nine

Michelle

I wasn't going to run him over, the big baby. I am making a point. He is not in control. I'm a grown woman and I will do whatever the hell I want. He steps away and I close my door. Watching him walk away, I take a deep, satisfied breath, buckle my seatbelt and set off.

I make it all of three feet before Drew's ridiculous truck rolls behind me and I have to slam on my brakes. I roll down my window and curse at him. "What the hell do you think you're doing?"

"Get in the truck," he barks at me.

"Get out of the way."

He shakes his head and holds my gaze. "You want to do this, we're doing it my way. You have two choices. Get in the truck or get back in the house."

I rev the tiny engine of my Mini. He cocks an eyebrow, calling my bluff. For a split second, I debate reversing right into the side of that stupid rusty truck of his. But I love my little car too much for that.

He breaks his stare and looks straight ahead. "Last chance, or I decide for you."

I duck back into my car and watch him in the rearview mirror. His head falls back against the seat and his hands tighten around the steering wheel. He looks tortured. *Good.*

I turn off my car and stomp around to the passenger side of his truck. I don't bother saying a word. He's won this round, but I refuse to admit it. He takes off down the road, the back end of his truck sliding and making me gasp. I hate the grin that lights up his face.

We drive for twenty minutes in ear-piercing silence. Both of us are staring out of the windshield, willing the other to cease existing. At least, that's what I'm doing, picturing a world without the likes of Drew Wright. A beautiful and blissful place.

Every second that rolls by makes me that much more confident he was lying. There is no tree. The road is fine. He came back because he wanted to. Because he wanted to be with me. I smile at the idea, the possibility of rejecting Drew with a viciousness that would make my dad question who he raised. Believe me, Drew has it coming. He did it to me first. He didn't just reject me — he humiliated me.

I hate that he caught me crying this morning. It wasn't over him, but it was *because* of him. He preys on every insecurity a geeky only child like me has. I never cried over my ex, Monte. Not even when I found out he cheated on me. *A lot.* He was a snake and a part of me always knew that. I ignored it because he was hot and rich and popular. It made me feel special that he wanted me, but I never pretended there was anything lasting behind it.

I thought Drew was different. *Boy, did he have me fooled.* He turned out to be the cruelest of them all. The one I didn't see coming. The one who made me feel like nothing. And now it is my turn. I am going to break him and enjoy every second of it.

"Feel free to admit you were lying." I keep my tone even and unaffected. He doesn't answer. "It's sweet really. That you had to make up some story about a tree. Just tell me —"

A yelp swallows my words as Drew slams on the brakes.

"You were saying?" he drawls, looking forward at the enormous tree across the road.

I hop out of the truck and slam the door, hoping he doesn't see the embarrassment coloring my cheeks. *Of course he didn't come back for me. Get over yourself, Michelle.*

My sneakers sink into the thick mud and I grip the side of the truck to pull my feet out of the muck. I take a deep breath and trek over to the massive tree. I look at the top and bottom of it. It covers the entire road and then some. There's no way to even drive around it. Drew was right — we're not going anywhere until we get this thing out of the way.

I'm trapped. With Drew Wright. The arrogant jerk who broke my heart. The sexy jock I let own my body last night. The mountain of a man who is laughing at me from his truck. I *hate* him. Every strong, thick, muscular *inch* of him.

I drop my hands to the fallen trunk and shove with everything I have. I grunt and heave. I push and prod. It doesn't budge. I lose it. I pound on it with my fists. I kick it with all the rage in my heart. I flail in a blind fury, screaming to the heavens. My lungs burn and my throat is sore when I finally settle.

"Feel better?" Drew's voice is full of arrogant condescension. I whip around and glare at him.

I take a step forward, determined to take out every ounce of anger I have on his smooth skin. He won't be laughing after I get my hands on him. Except the world hates me and when I step forward, my shoe doesn't come with me. The mud seeps into my sock, the coolness oozing between my toes when I unwittingly plant it into the deep mud.

Drew's laugh grows louder from the truck. Anger surges through my body. I whip around, grabbing at my shoe and tugging with everything I have. It comes loose easier than I anticipated, sending me sprawling backward on my ass in the thick mud. I hold my shoe up in victory as the wet splat of my back hitting the mud fills my ears.

"Oh, shit," Drew calls behind me. The truck door slams shut and squishy footsteps close in. "You hurt?" he asks, kneeling over me. *As if he cares.*

I pinch my eyes shut and wallow in the mud and my own ruin. I shake my head, more in disbelief at my life than in answer to his question. I crack one eye open and catch the sight of his scruffy jaw and adorable dimples. It's not fair that someone so evil is so ruggedly beautiful.

I sit up and shove him. I'm quick enough to catch him off guard and he topples over next to me in the mud with a gasped, "Shit."

I can't stop the wicked laugh that barrels out of me. His front is coated in mud, chin to shins.

"What the hell was that for?" he asks, sitting back on his heels.

I smirk. "For being you. Trust me, you had it coming."

He shakes his head, a smile forcing its way onto those sexy full lips.

Chapter Ten

Drew

Seeing a smile ghost across Michelle's lips for the first time in the twenty-four hours we've been trapped together is almost enough to make up for being coated in thick mud. *Almost.*

I scoop up a handful of the gritty stuff and chuck it at her. The mud ball hits her square between her perky tits and splatters up to her face. Now it's my turn to laugh.

"Oh, no you didn't!" she screeches before launching that nimble body at me.

I barely have time to brace myself before she scrambles on top of me. She moves with purpose, pinning me down, and I let her. Her hands on my shoulders press my back into the ground, making sure I've got mud coating three-hundred-and-sixty degrees of my body. She straddles me and I dig my fingers into her hips like a sculptor molding clay, firm but cautious.

My mind flashes back to last night, to pinning her down and seeing the desire surging through her. She's got that same look in her eyes now, that defiant glint that tells me she wants me but she doesn't need me. The look that gets me hard.

She rolls her hips, riding me in slow, controlled movements. I'm not even sure she knows she's doing it. "You belong down here. A pig rolling in the mud."

"You're down here with me, princess." I lift my ass out of the mud and grind up into her. "And I don't hear you complaining."

Realizing I didn't kiss her last night, I drop my gaze to her lips. It wasn't a conscious choice. I was consumed with owning every other inch of her, but I didn't need the intimacy of her lips on mine. Out here, getting filthy under the summer sun, I wonder if she still tastes like cherries.

I reach up to her face, my mud-coated hand leaving a streak on her jaw at the caress. She stares down at me, pausing for half a breath before batting my hand away and popping up.

"Please. There is no part of this I'm enjoying." She tenses, waiting for me to call her out on her bullshit.

I don't let her obvious denial rile me up. We both know she enjoyed my fingers, tongue and cock plenty last night. I follow her to the passenger side of the truck and pin her in against the door.

"Can I help you?" she asks, sarcasm lashing at me with each syllable.

I lean down and whisper, "You're filthy."

Her back presses against my chest when she takes a deep breath. I push away from her.

"You're not getting in my truck like that." I let disgust coat my words.

"Exactly what do you suggest?" Her voice is breathy but strong.

I strip my shirt off over my head and toss it in the back of the truck with a wet thud. I know I've got a nice body. I'm not a vain asshole like her boyfriend Monte. This body is my meal ticket. It's a tool I've spent most of my life sharpening. Being chiseled like a god is a nice bonus, but not the goal.

Her eyes drink me up, lingering on every inch of muscle before devouring the next. She can hate me all she wants, but it doesn't stop her from wanting me. I'd bet my signing bonus that she's getting wet at the sight of my bare chest. I strut around the front of the truck, unbuttoning my pants along the way. I open the driver's side door, knowing she can see what I'm doing through the passenger window, and let my mud-coated jeans drop to my ankles with a smirk.

"Why are you always getting naked?" she asks, trying to sound unaffected.

I lift myself up to the bench seat, slip off my boots and toss them into the bed with a heavy thud. My jeans follow behind. Sliding in, I rest an arm on the back of the seat, pretending I'm comfortable behind the wheel in nothing but my boxers.

"Some of us aren't prudes," I tell her. I'm full of shit. My heart is racing and I feel exposed. But she looks even more uncomfortable, so it's worth it.

"I'm not taking my clothes off." She crosses her arms and scowls.

"Suit yourself." I gesture to the bed of the truck. "Your chariot awaits."

"Back there?" she scoffs, indignant as fuck.

"Naked in here or plant your muddy ass back there. Your choice. I don't give a shit." I cringe at my own words. My sisters would have my ass for being such a dick. I'm not usually an asshole, but Michelle Anders has a way of bringing out my baser nature. *My brutish side.* I chuckle at the thought. *Guess her nickname isn't that far off.* "Hurry up, princess, or you'll be walking." I start the engine.

I hate myself a little for the way she makes me act. But I hate her more. She has it coming.

"I'm not taking my clothes off," she declares. I nod back to the bed of the truck. "And I'm not riding in the back like a farm animal."

I don't look at her when I shift into drive. "Walking it is then," I call out. I only roll forward a few inches, not actually stepping on the gas.

Her tiny hands slap on the doorframe and she gasps. "Wait!"

I slide my foot to the brake pedal and make a show of jerking to a stop. I turn and take in the sight of her. Lips drawn in a tight line. Eyebrows pinched together, causing a deep wrinkle to slice through her forehead. Round eyes narrowed into slits.

I cock an unaffected eyebrow and wait.

She maintains eye contact as she strips off her shirt. I refuse to look down at her soft tits and the hard nipples I'm sure are peeking through her bra. She rips open the door, unbuttons her pants and slides them down her milky thighs. She spins and hops up onto the seat like I did. Her pants, socks, shoes and shirt are tossed into the back of the truck. I take off again, keeping my eyes off her naked body.

Chapter Eleven

Michelle

The drive back to the lake house is quiet. Drew watches the road with a smug grin and I seethe in a controlled rage. Andrew Wright is the biggest asshole I've ever met. I don't know how I could have ever thought any different. Hate isn't a strong enough word for what I feel for him. Loathing. Disgust. Contempt. None are strong enough. He's just the worst human being in existence.

I'm out of his truck the second we're parked and I storm straight into a shower. I turn the water on to just below scalding. He's unbearable and irritatingly irresistible. The idea of riding him like the wild animal he is has me sliding my hand down between my thighs.

Stop it!

I refuse to touch myself to thoughts of that unworthy brute. Somehow he'd know and he'd win. I refuse to give him the satisfaction. Instead, I grab my loofa and scrub my body raw. Mud circles the drain, but the memory of straddling him in the woods doesn't wash away.

Out of the shower, I get dressed in a simple red wrap dress with white polka dots. It's feminine and sweet. My armor. I put my makeup back on, making my eyes pop and my lips shimmer. *My war paint.*

Feeling more in control of myself, I call Elizabeth.

"Hey, Michelle," she answers with a shy smile.

"Hey." I blow out a deep breath. "We've got a new problem."

I describe the whole thing in painful detail. The disaster muddy road that my little Mini would never survive. The giant tree blocking the only way in or out. The stubborn jackass who made me strip to avoid being abandoned on the side of the road.

"That's crazy, babe. What are the odds?" Elizabeth sympathizes before darting her eyes up to the right like she's actually calculating the odds of me being trapped in this ridiculous situation with the worst person imaginable.

"Can you call the city to come remove the tree or something?" I plead.

She shakes her head and refocuses on me. "Sure. I'm on it. Don't worry. I'll get it all sorted."

"Thanks, Lizbit." I hang up and feel a little better. At least I have an ally in all of this.

My stomach rumbles and I will myself not to be as hungry. Going to the kitchen means dealing with the ogre of a man. *So what?* He doesn't own the kitchen! I'm not staying locked away in my room for however long it takes to get that tree out of the way. I have just as much right to this lake house as he does. *More.* I was here first, after all.

I pull my shoulders back and stalk into the kitchen with purpose. Anxiety prickles my skin and my heart pounds. I can sense him on the couch, but I refuse to look at him. I pretend he doesn't exist. To me, he doesn't. He's not worth a minute of my time.

I clatter around in the kitchen, waiting for him to notice me, to say something. He doesn't. He's ignoring me. It's aggravating. I'm the one who's supposed to be ignoring him. I'm desperate for him to ask me what's wrong so I can tell him to go to hell, but he doesn't. Every minute that ticks by, I'm more desperate for his attention. That's not fair.

I take a bite of the peanut butter and jelly sandwich I made and let myself look at him. He's reclined on the couch, a book in his hands and a contented look on his face. The sweetness of the jelly turns sour in my mouth with my frustration.

"No pictures? I didn't realize you *could* read," I snip. It's childish, but I'm not above picking a fight.

His face is unchanged. He licks a finger and turns a page. "Hard to make the dean's list without being able to read," he replies, unaffected.

The dean's list? To do that he must have maintained at least a 3.5 grade point average, while turning heads on the football field. I swallow hard, resisting the compulsion to be impressed.

"Guess even dogs can learn tricks," I quip, taking another bite of my sandwich even though my appetite is waning.

"Arf," he barks out, a wicked grin on his lips.

I pinch my eyes closed and force down a smile. My phone vibrating in my back pocket makes me jump.

"I've got good news and bad news," Elizabeth starts in as soon as I answer.

At the sound of her voice, Drew puts his book down and crosses over to the kitchen. He's wearing fresh clothes — another pair of jeans and a T-shirt. It's discount-rack-at-Target-level basic, but his body fills out every inch in a way that doesn't need designer labels. He's a simple guy, something I could appreciate if I didn't hate him. My dad loves to spoil his only child and my mom loves to shop, so I've always had nice things. But I've never understood why people like my ex are so obsessed with the status symbols. They're just things.

Drew's eyes find mine, the glint in them enough to let me know he caught me checking him out. I huff out an annoyed breath. "You're not as sexy as you think."

His lopsided smile and a stupid little wink are his way of saying, "Yes, I am."

"Good news first. I need it," I tell Elizabeth while scowling at Drew.

"Good news is the storm blew itself out, so no more rain. The next few days are supposed to be absolutely beautiful. Perfect days to be at the lake house!" Her voice is full of forced cheerfulness that puts me on high alert.

"And the bad news?"

Elizabeth sucks a breath in through her teeth. "It's a private road, so the city won't come fix it. I had to hire a company to remove the tree."

That doesn't sound too bad. Expensive, but Elizabeth's family can handle it, I'm sure. Then it hits me.

"When?" I ask.

"That's the thing..." Elizabeth trails off.

"Elizabeth...how long?" My voice is hard. I can feel Drew's judgmental gaze on me and it just makes me more anxious to get out of here.

"A week."

"A *week*!" Drew and I yell in unison. The only thing we both agree on is spending a week together is out of the question.

"I guess that storm did a lot of damage across the county. They're swamped. No pun intended."

"Did you tell them it was a matter of life and death?" I look up at Drew, my eyes wide and wild. One of us will kill the other if we're stuck here together for another week.

"I know this is a bit of a nightmare, but there's food and power. No one is hurt or in danger, so they say they can't move me up the list at all. I'm so sorry, Michelle."

I know she is. Elizabeth is a sweetheart. She was helping me out by letting me stay here. It's not her fault I'm now trapped with a brute. I feel like a crappy friend for making her stress about something that isn't her fault. She's done everything she can.

"It'll be okay." I force positivity into my voice.

"Fuckin' peachy," Drew groans.

I stare daggers at him and shake my head with force. He shrugs and slips into the kitchen.

"Seriously, Elizabeth. This isn't your fault. We'll be fine. If I kill him, I'll make sure it's out in the woods so I don't stain any of the furniture."

Drew barks out a laugh behind me and I smile at the thought of wrapping my slender fingers around his thick throat.

Chapter Twelve

Drew

I've never tried so hard to ignore someone in my life. Michelle is tiny, but I'm aware of every move she makes. She struts around the living room like she's making a point. She keeps her distance without making it look like she is. The princess is determined to establish dominance in our little war for territory.

If we're stuck here together for an entire fucking week, neither of us is willing to cede control of the common spaces. Still, being in the same room with her is torture. I read the same page in my book about a dozen times before I decided to turn the damn page. *Can't have her thinking I can't read.*

My phone has chimed about a dozen times since I logged into the wi-fi and I know it must be my sisters blowing up our group chat. I don't bother checking it. Chances are it's another overly explicit conversation about Samantha's pregnancy hormones. I'm excited as fuck to be an uncle, but I don't need to know about her engorged *anything*! I swear, some days they forget I have a dick.

"Aren't you a popular brute. Going to answer your *girlfriend*?" Michelle spits out.

"Jealous?" I tease. She scoffs, not looking up from her tablet. Her face goes pale and she squeezes her eyes tight. She's not fond of being the other woman. "No need to get your panties in a twist, princess. I don't have a girlfriend."

Michelle lets out a haughty sigh, her heart-shaped lips pinching together in an angry pucker and that deep line forming between her eyebrows. Hit a nerve, I see.

I pull my phone out and scroll through the messages. My sisters are trying to arrange a dinner this weekend. I shoot back a text saying I can't make it.

"Of course not. That would require loyalty," Michelle mumbles.

"Sleeping around is not *my* style. Like you have any idea how to fucking spell *loyalty*," I snap at her. The fucking nerve of this chick.

My eyes burn into her across the living room. When my oldest sister initiates a video call, it takes everything in me not to escape to my room. I know she is going to give me shit about this stupid dinner and I don't want Michelle to hear me get pussy whipped. Unfortunately, that would mean running away.

I stay put and accept the call with an annoyed, "What, Sam?"

"Whoa. Check the attitude, baby brother," Samantha's loud voice echoes across the living room. "What crawled up your butt?"

Michelle snickers and I know she can hear my obnoxious sister.

"Nothing," I mutter.

"Right. Whatever. Why aren't you answering your phone and what's this crap about you not coming to dinner this weekend?" Samantha is about ten years older than me and the pushiest woman I've ever met. She doesn't think she's my mom — she thinks she's my boss.

"I'm out of town and I don't have cell service. Just the wi-fi." I keep it vague. I didn't tell my family I took off for the week, needing some space to clear my head. I love them, but they're a lot to handle.

I don't look up, but I can tell Michelle is paying attention by the sound of her tabletbeing tossed down on the coffee table.

"Out of town? Where are you?" Samantha asks, like she has any right to know.

"Just out of town. Don't worry about it."

"He's hiding out at a lake house in Palmetto," Michelle chimes in.

My head pops up and I grind my teeth. Michelle doesn't know the shit storm she just kicked up. Then again, with the smug look on her face, maybe she does.

"Who was that?" Sam asks, her demanding voice full of curious excitement.

"No one."

Michelle chuckles and I've had enough. I stand, grab my book and head out to the porch.

"I can't talk right now. I'll call you back later." I hang up on Samantha only to have our group chat blow up for the next few hours with ridiculous attempts to get the gossip about Michelle. My sisters threaten and blackmail trying to get me to spill the story. I don't. It's complicated.

I liked Michelle. A lot. If I'm honest, I was falling a little bit in love with her. Then I realized she wasn't who she was pretending to be. She was using me. Now I hate her. And I'm stuck with her. *See? Complicated.*

After the video call from hell, the day wastes away with Michelle and I both determined not to acknowledge that the other exists. We're ghosts in that house, floating around each other. I ignore the way my skin tingles when she's close enough to touch.

It's two o'clock in the morning and I can't sleep. Every time I close my eyes, I picture Michelle in those booty shorts she has the nerve to call pajamas. My cock is hard and eager, images of her pinned under me haunting my waking dreams.

As I slide my hand into my boxers, a scream pierces the darkness. My blood runs cold and I'm frozen in place. The second scream has me out of bed and charging toward Michelle's room.

My muscles carry me through the empty house without thought. My stomach is churning. The bitter taste of adrenaline fills my mouth. My hands are coiled into tight fists. My heart is surging in my chest, desperate to reach her.

I throw open her door without bothering to knock. I flick on the light and charge into the room, searching for the guy I'm going to beat to death with my bare hands for making her scream like that.

The room is empty except for the petite woman writhing on the bed, crying in muffled terror. My heart splits open at the sound. I'm across the room in half a heartbeat and reaching for her.

I grip her shoulders and give a hard shake. I call her name loud enough to wake her up. Her eyes snap open on another panting scream. She pulls away and her arms come up in front of her, like she's protecting herself from a blow. When none comes, her gaze searches the room in a wild panic. She takes heaving breaths like she's been running for her life. She scurries up the bed away from me and buries her head in her hands.

"It's all right. It was a dream," I try to reassure her, but my voice is still rough.

Her shoulders shake and she begins to weep, long sorrowful howls racking her tiny body. Without thinking, I sit down on the bed next to her. Leaning against the headboard, I lift her into my lap. Her whole body tenses at the touch, but I don't stop. I cradle her against my chest, wrapping her in my arms and squeezing tight.

"You're safe," I whisper in her ear. "I won't let anything hurt you."

I've lost track of time when she begins to calm, her breath coming in slow and even inhales, her body stiff but not tense.

"I was mugged." Her shaky voice rings in my ear. My arms tighten around her in reflex. She nuzzles into my chest and continues. "I was fifteen, walking home from a party at a friend's house. It was late and dark, but we live in such a safe neighborhood I wasn't even paying attention." She pulls in a sharp breath and holds it. I count to ten in my head. "Something slammed into me from behind and pushed me up against a fence. He had a hood pulled down over his face. I never saw him. But I saw the knife. He shoved it into my chest and told me to give him everything I had."

She pushes her fingers into her sternum so hard the tips go white. I'm glad I can't see the pain on her face at reliving the memory. I might tear the house down.

"I was lucky, I guess. He could've done...*anything*, but he didn't. Just took the money and ran." The wobble in her voice gives it a pitiful whimsy. "I didn't scream. I didn't cry. I didn't make a *peep*. I just stared at the point of the knife cutting into my Calvin Klein top."

She goes quiet again. I brush her dark hair back off her shoulder and run my hand down the goosebumps on her arms. When I fail to smooth them away with my warm palm, I shuffle us around to slide under the covers and flick off the light, never loosening my hold on her.

Her sharp words cut through the darkness.

"I don't dream about him. I dream about the knife. It slices into me again and again, but I can't scream. When I try nothing comes out." She breaks down again, her body feeling so small curled in against me and shaking with her hefty tears.

I hold her for the rest of the night, cradled snug in my arms, whispering reassuring words to her and making promises I can't keep.

Michelle finally falls asleep as the sun begins to warm the room with dawn light. I hold her to me, wanting to make sure she knows she's safe, until exhaustion pulls me under.

When I wake up, the bed is cold, the room is bright and Michelle is gone.

Chapter Thirteen

Michelle

It's been years since I've had a night terror that bad, where the fear is crippling and the panic is suffocating. It took me right back to that night, to feeling helpless. *Weak. Insignificant.*

I clung to Drew like he was my lifeline. I've never been so grateful for another human being. His deep voice promising he'd keep me safe meant the world. I believed him. I shouldn't. I can't trust him. But he sounded so earnest and he held me so tight, I never doubted him.

Everything is different in the bright light of day. After the fear fades, his arms don't feel safe. They're a warm and welcoming trap. I can't rely on guys like him. They'll tell a girl one thing, make sweet promises then shatter her heart.

I know him. I've seen who he really is. A selfish, spiteful and cruel brute. I liked him. A lot. I think I was even falling a little bit in love with him. Then he humiliated me. I'll never be able to trust a man like him again. I hate myself for being weak, for telling him the truth about my dreams. There can be no chinks in my armor when it comes to Andrew Wright. He'll weasel his way in and tear me apart. That knowledge alleviates any guilt I should feel about prying myself out of his protective grip and sneaking out of the bedroom.

I'm sipping coffee and hardening my heart when he makes his appearance. He's adorable in wrinkled pajamas and wild bed hair. I shove the attraction for him deep down and bury it under my bitterness.

"Morning." His voice is thick with sleep. "How are you doing?" he asks as if he's genuinely concerned. I won't let myself believe it.

"I'm fine." I keep my voice even and detached. "Thank you for your abnormal kindness last night. I'm sure it must've left a bad taste in your mouth."

The coffee mug that had almost made its way to his full lips slams down on the kitchen counter, splashing the hot black liquid across his fingers. He swears under his breath and shakes off the pain. "Excuse me?" His voice is cold and hard as a steel blade.

I clear my throat. "I said thank you."

"No, you didn't. You gave me a backhanded compliment like a passive-aggressive brat." His words cut into me, but I refuse to flinch at the wound.

"No. I said thank you. But doing something vaguely human doesn't change who you are, what you did or the fact that I *hate* you for it." The words taste like a lie and my mouth twists at their venom.

"Fine. Next time I'll let you scream into the darkness and I'll sleep like a baby." He takes a sip of his coffee and struts down the hallway toward his room. Over his shoulder he adds, "And for the record I still fucking *hate* you too."

It isn't his words that hurt, but the way he says them. He believes them. He hates me. He used to be someone I cared about. Someone I thought I knew. Last night I caught a glimpse of the guy I hoped he was, the one that I could fall hard for. I shouldn't care, but his words torture me for the rest of the day.

He has no right to hate me.

Drew ignores me with intense precision. He makes himself lunch without looking at me. He takes a swim in the lake without a word. He sits on the couch playing a loud, constantly chiming game on his phone — that is driving me insane — without looking at me. Every hour that ticks by makes my eye twitch and skin prickle. The tension has me coiled like a spring. He's as fresh as a spring breeze.

I can't take it anymore. After dinner, I storm off to my room and slam the door shut. Throwing myself onto the bed, I let out a frustrated breath. I grab my noise-canceling headphones and shuffle my good mood playlist, trying to distract myself. I've never met someone so infuriating.

How can he drive me crazy by ignoring me?

I should be ecstatic. But instead I'm a twisted mess of mixed emotions. I want to smash a lamp over his thick skull. I want to tackle him to the ground, straddle him and wrap my hands around his neck until he begs me for mercy. I want him under me, helpless and pleading. I want him to know I'm small but not weak. I can make him beg.

I close my eyes and picture my hands pressing his broad shoulders into the ground, the tortured look on his face when I swirl my hips over his hardening length.

I hate myself for wanting him, but I can't control it. My head and my body are not on the same page. I don't think they're even reading the same book.

My nipples begin to bud against my bra, so I unhook it and tug it off with my shirt in one motion. Lying back on my bed, I squeeze my thighs together and twist my nipples, imagining Drew's callused fingers dragging over them. I hum to myself and let one hand slide down my stomach to the button of my shorts. I flick it open, Drew's deep voice pleading for more in my head. I tell him to beg. I imagine finally having his rapt attention, and it's intoxicating.

I kick my shorts aside and rub myself, imagining the friction of grinding down onto Drew with teasing strokes. My mouth falls open and my breath comes in long pants. I want him between my thighs. I whisper his name in a stern command, telling him to touch me.

I'm so lost in my desire I could swear I feel the ghosting tease of his fingertips on the inside of my thigh. I bite my lip and moan at the sensation, my hips lifting off the bed and into the touch. The caress turns into a firm grip and a deep moan breaks through the music in my headphones.

I rip them off my ears, snap my eyes open and gasp at the sight of Drew sitting on the edge of the bed, one hand gripping the sensitive skin at the inside of my thigh, the other rubbing his hard dick through his pants. The hunger in his eyes is more aggressive and wanton than even in my daydream.

I shoot up and pull away from him. My face burns with embarrassment. My heart is stampeding and I'm gasping. I cling to the fury I should feel at him sneaking into my room and watching me in such an intimate moment, but all I see is the bulge he's stroking in a long, slow, punishing motion. I lick my lips and swallow. When the desire to taste him hits me, I shake my head violently and force myself back into reality. I cover my bare breast with one arm and shove him away with the other.

"What the hell do you think you're doing?" I screech, indignant. "This is my room. You have no right—"

"You called my name," he blurts out with controlled rage. Or is it lust?

"I *what*?" I don't believe him. I didn't call his name. *Not out loud.* I couldn't have.

"You called my name. Moaned it. I thought you were having another bad dream…" His eyes lap up every inch of my naked skin. I refuse to cower. I'm nearly naked, but I will not let him see my insecurity or shame at being found touching myself to the thought of him. If I called his name, there's no point in denying it now.

"Ever heard of knocking?"

"I did. You didn't answer. So, I came in and saw you…"

He has the decency not to finish that sentence.

"And you thought you might as well cop a feel?" I stare at him, refusing to back down. He meets my challenge. The tension that's surrounded us for the last few days simmers between loathing and desire.

"You *told* me to touch you," he answers.

I bite my lip, turned on by the idea of this beast of a man bowing to my commands.

"Since when do you do what I say?" I jut my chin out, challenging him.

"Since I wanted it too," he confesses, his jaw tight and his teeth grinding. He hates himself for admitting it, but we both know it's the only way forward now. We can't spend the next week ignoring each other without this painful and undeniable appetite boiling over.

I drop my arm and Drew's gaze falls to my bare chest with a low moan.

"Take your clothes off," I tell him, thankful I keep my voice detached.

He pulls his eyes back up to mine and we stare into each other. A silent stalemate is formed in those few seconds, the admission that neither of us can walk away. Neither of us wants to.

He rises, his tall and hard body towering over me. I watch as he slowly strips, peeling each article of clothing off just like I instructed. He stands naked in front of me, a fierce vulnerability etched into his face. He nods to me, asking for his next task.

"Lie down. On your back." My voice shakes, hunger making it unsteady.

Drew circles the bed and lies down next to me. His hard length surges up to his stomach. I lean over him, raking my nails up the inside of his thigh hard enough to leave red scratches in their wake. He groans. I'm not gentle, but we both know this is how it has to be. How we both want it.

"Do you want me to touch you?" I ask. He nods. "Tell me. Tell me how much you want me." I trace a finger up the thick vein on the underside of his dick and his eyes slam shut.

"I want you to wrap those soft lips around my cock and slide them down my shaft until I hit the back of your throat." His voice is a deep, sexy rasp.

I lean forward and do just what he asks, taking him in my mouth and enjoying the taste of his pre-cum on my tongue. A moan slips out of me and Drew jerks his hips up to meet my mouth.

"Fuck," he grits out. He fists the back of my panties and rips them down as far as they will go, where my knees hit the mattress. He slides two fingers along my folds. "You're so fucking wet, princess."

I pull back and stare down at him. He's holding his breath, like he's nervous. I bet he's praying using the nickname I hate hasn't spoiled the game.

"I'm not your princess," I snarl. His mouth opens, but I slap a hand over it. I don't want his words. Tonight, I want his body.

I slide off my panties, climb over and settle on top of him. I lay a hand on each of his hard pecs and lean back. I glide over his hard cock, getting off on the feel of him bucking into me. When I try to lift off him, he grips my hips and pulls me back down.

"I want to be inside you."

"You think a brute like you deserves such a reward?" I taunt him with a swivel of my hips. The sensation of his hard cock against my swollen clit makes me moan.

He sits up and takes one of my aching nipples into his mouth. "I know how you want it. Hard. I can give that to you." He bites down on my nipple, sending waves of pleasure down to my core.

"Condom," I demand.

He groans. It's not sexual. It's exasperated. "I don't have one."

I shove him back onto the mattress and climb off. He's too surprised to catch me in time. I'm across the room, wrapping myself in my satin robe before he manages to mutter, "You can't be serious?"

I cross my arms and glare at him. "As a heart attack." I'm on birth control, but after finding out the relationship with Monte I thought was monogamous wasn't, I'm not going to take any chances. With anyone.

Drew rolls off the bed and charges to my bedroom door. Nearly tearing it off the hinges, he turns back to point a finger at me and says, "Don't move."

I yawn and he leaves with a sigh, still completely naked. I bite back a smile. The sound of cabinets banging and muttered curses trails through the house. I startle at the sound of the front door slamming. He's back in two minutes, an unopened box of condoms clutched in his fist.

"None in the house. But I remembered these were in the truck." He looks down at the box and a shy blush creeps up past the stubble on his rugged face. "Gift from the guys when I was drafted," he explains.

I shake my head, realizing he charged out to his truck butt naked. He's determined, I'll give him that. He clears his throat and traces up my body with his hungry eyes.

"Take off the robe."

I humor him, slowly. I hold the robe closed after I untie it, letting each shoulder pop out before it drops to the floor. Eyes locked on me — *no, I didn't move* — Drew tears open the box with his teeth, looking downright feral. He pumps his still-hard cock twice and rolls on the condom.

Without a word, he lunges for the bed and lies down. He slips his hands under his head and stares up at the ceiling.

"I'm ready," he declares.

I can't hold back the small laugh that shuffles up my throat. He's cocky and yet too damn adorable to resist. The rapid rise and fall of his broad chest and his locked jaw show he's not nearly as casual as he's trying to pretend.

Straddling him again, I guide his cock to my opening and slide down onto him. He digs his fingers into my hips and he moans. The pleasure is so intense it's nearly painful.

Chapter Fourteen

Drew

She's right—she's not a princess. She's a warrior. A brutal and unforgiving fighter and I've never seen anything sexier. I dig my fingers into her thighs like a drowning man reaching for the shore. I'm not controlling anything, but I'm desperate to hold on to her. She's riding me, using my cock to get herself off.

The swivel of her hips drives me deeper inside her. It's hot that she's not intimidated by me, that she's confident enough to take what she wants. I'm a huge guy, have been since I was a kid. Most girls are timid and skittish around me, like if they say something wrong, I'll gobble them up.

Not Michelle.

She's challenged me from the first moment, trying to tell me Wonder Woman could take Captain Marvel in a fight. A sexy smart chick who reads comic books? I thought I'd won the fucking relationship lottery. Turns out, if something is too good to be true, it usually is.

The reminder of who she is has that familiar anger flooding my veins. Gripping hard, I pull her down into me while I lift my hips up to meet her. She gasps and looks down at me. *That's right, princess. I'm going to get what I want too.*

It's no longer sex—it's a battle. Both of us struggle to control the pace, the position and our own climaxes.

"You're going to come on my cock," I tell her, my voice thick and raspy. She moans, a half-annoyed, half-excited sound. "You're close."

"So are you," she pants.

I smile at the challenge in her voice. "I want to feel you come first. Feel that tight pussy clench around me."

The dirty talk pushes her over the edge. She's muttering unintelligible swear words while she rides out her orgasm on top of me. The sight sends me over the edge. I don't think I've come so hard in my entire life.

She slows to a leisurely pace as we both catch our breath. I relax my grip and stroke her thigh with my thumbs, feeling her soft smooth skin under my thick, rough fingers. With a final satisfied hum, she bends forward, swan diving into my chest until her forehead hits my sternum and her silky black hair falls down along my ribs.

I slide my hand into her hair and cup the back of her neck. I place a gentle kiss on the top of her head and breathe in the sweet smell of her. It's intimate and tender, something I don't realize until I've already done it. Must be all the post-orgasm endorphins making me act like an idiot.

I expect her to say something snide or to pull back and bolt. Something to remind us both we hate each other. Instead, she lets out a satisfied coo, straightens her legs and tucks her tiny body in against my side. Guess she's high on those endorphins too. Her head is on my shoulder, her warm breath tickling my chest. Her front is sandwiched against my side, a leg tossed over my stomach. We're cuddling and she's snoring within minutes. *This woman is insane.*

Chapter Fifteen

Michelle

I wake up coiled around Drew for the third morning in a row. He's broad and warm and surprisingly comfortable for a guy coated in so much muscle. Still, the realization that I'm cuddling my enemy has my stomach churning and my mouth going dry. I unwrap my legs and pull myself away from him.

I climb into the shower, letting the warm water wash away all my unease. *How did we get here?*

I've had sex with him.

Twice. And last night I didn't even have the alcohol to blame. I'm drawn to him, my body responding to him in a way I crave. My mind is swirling like the water circling the drain when I hear the click of the bathroom door.

I don't move, or even look up when Drew climbs into the massive rain shower. I stifle the moan when he presses his hard chest into my back and wraps his strong arms around my waist. He nips at my shoulder, not hard enough to hurt, but firm enough to know it's a reprimand.

"I'm getting sick of waking up alone when that's not how I fell asleep." He grazes my earlobe with his tongue, sending tingles down my spine.

I lean back into him, dropping my head against his shoulder. Letting go of our past and avoiding the question of our future, I focus on the feel of him behind me now. How large he is, how he engulfs me. How good it feels to be wrapped up in him.

"You're so big," I hear myself mumble.

Drew grinds into me, his hard length sliding against my ass, slick from the water running between our bodies. He hums in approval and I shake my head.

"I didn't mean *that*," I tell him with a chuckle. "You're big everywhere. You make me feel so small."

"You are small." He strokes my stomach in lazy circles with his thumbs.

"I'm average."

His chest rumbles. "Far from it, princess." He kisses my neck and glides one of his large hands south between my thighs.

I bite my lip and close my eyes. "I don't want this," I moan.

His body stiffens behind me and his hand freezes. He begins to pull back, to pull away, and I realize he misunderstood me. I grab his hands and keep them locked around me, shifting my weight back against him.

"I don't *want* to want this, but I do. I can't help it. It's wrong, but I want you," I tell him, unable to hold back the simple truth. My voice is a broken whisper. If he weren't pressed against me, the water would have drowned out my confession. I wish it had. I feel bare and vulnerable, not trusting him not to hurt me.

"So wrong, it's right," Drew murmurs against my skin. He slides his hand back between my thighs. Pressing his leg into my knee, he encourages me to lift it onto the small seat in the corner of the shower. I do, opening myself up to him. I lean back and let him take my weight, trusting him not to drop me.

His hard length is pressed against me, and as desperate as I am to have him inside me again, I don't trust him enough for that yet.

"Condom," I moan when he positions himself at my entrance.

Not pulling back, he grumbles, "How the fuck are you the only woman in the state not on birth control?"

His harsh tone chaffs against my raw nerves. "Of course I'm on birth control. Not that it's any of your business," I snip.

"Then why—" His voice cuts off. He rips his body away from mine and I stumble back, nearly falling without him to brace me. Cold air rushes between us and I shiver at the loss of his body against mine. "That's fucking rich," he growls with an agitated edge.

"Excuse me?" I ask, spinning to watch his retreating form. I don't know what happened. A minute ago, we were connected, lost in a delicate bubble of soap and steam. Now, he's glaring at me with smoldering hatred.

"I said that's rich. *You* making *me* wear a condom." He snatches a towel off the shelf and wraps it around his still hard length. It barely covers his wide frame, a slit up his thick thigh drawing my attention and keeping me eager for him.

I shake my head, still not understanding his anger. "Why is that so funny?"

"You are worried about catching something from me?" Drew snaps. "You've slept with half the damn football team and I haven't been with anyone in almost a year."

His accusation slams into me and I brace myself against the shower wall. I don't register his confession. I'm too angry at his egotistical rant.

"You are such an asshole!" I shout, turning off the shower and grabbing a towel to cover my body.

"At least I'm an honest one." He levels me with a glare.

A sarcastic cackle rumbles out of my mouth. "Honest? You're honestly a misinformed jackass who's too busy believing his own idiotic gossip to bother thinking about the people he's hurting." Angry tears tumble out of my eyes and I hope he can't tell the difference between them and the water dripping out of my hair. I storm past him, charging out of the bathroom with fury pumping through my body. I grab the first set of clothes I put my hands on, eager to have something solid between my body and his.

He steps out of the bathroom in nothing but that ridiculous too-small towel, droplets sliding down his glistening body. But I'm too angry to want him. Hate has replaced every ounce of desire. I'd sooner murder him than sleep with him.

His eyes are studying me, watching my every move with a curious confusion. I'm an exhibit in a zoo, here for him to gawk at. I'm desperate to hide how easily he can still hurt me. I hate myself for giving him that power again.

"Get out of my room," I shout.

"With pleasure."

Chapter Sixteen

Drew

Michelle is a good actress. Manipulative women have to be. I almost thought I'd hurt her, but she's just angry I called her out on her bullshit. She wants to pretend she's this sweet, innocent little thing when we both know she's not. She's vicious.

I storm back to my room and slam the door hard enough to rattle the windows.

"Fuck!" I shout into the empty space. My mind is a clouded mess and my muscles burn with the need to hit something. Break something. What I wouldn't give to be on the field right now.

I throw on a pair of gym shorts and my running shoes. I need to burn off this energy before I bring the house down around us.

I turn off my brain and focus on my feet churning up the miles along the lake. It's already hot, the morning sun beating down on my bare chest, but I push myself harder. I haven't eaten or had anything to drink since last night. I'm getting faint, but I don't stop. I run until my head clears. I run until I don't think about Michelle. Until I can't think about anything besides willing myself to keep moving. Until I'm so exhausted I can barely stand.

I stumble back into the house over two hours later, my lungs burning and my legs shaking. I head straight to the sink and down two glasses of cool water. I'm dripping with sweat, but I don't bother showering before I find myself some food.

In the kitchen, making grilled cheese for lunch, I am painfully aware of Michelle sitting in the living room. She hasn't said a word since I walked out of her bedroom. I hope she's got the chick version of blue balls.

We're back to pretending to ignore each other. I know she's as aware of my presence as I am of hers. Every time I slam a cabinet or bang a pan her shoulders tense and her lips purse.

It's a sick fucking game. A passive-aggressive challenge.

I'm staring down at the melting cheese in my pan, focusing all my energy on not thinking about Michelle, when I hear her phone ring and ping and vibrate for five solid minutes. Each time she ignores it, she gets more agitated. I'm not stupid enough to ask her who it is. *Besides, it's not like I even care.*

"Fuck off," she huffs, slamming the phone down on the coffee table. Now I'm interested.

After another five minutes and half a dozen more pings, she finally answers it.

"What the hell do you want, dickhead?"

My spatula freezes at the harshness in her voice. She hates me, and I've been on the receiving end of some of her sharpest jabs, but the sheer disgust dripping off her words now is a whole new experience. She sounds like she'd happily tear the person on the other end limb from limb. I'm both turned on and terrified. I'm also curious as fuck to know who is on the other end of that line.

"Ha!" She barks out a dry chuckle. "And why the hell do I care?"

Silence fills the massive house and I hold my breath.

"You got *exactly* what you deserve, Monte. You're a cheating piece of shit. I hope the steroids shrivel up your balls and an STD makes your dick rot and fall off. Don't. Ever. Contact. Me. Again."

My blood runs cold and I burn the grilled cheese.

Monte. As in Zachary Montgomery. My ex-teammate and her boyfriend. Or ex-boyfriend, I guess. He was caught not only doping, but paying a guy at the lab to cover it up. If that weren't enough proof he's an asshole, he also framed Austin just because Austin kicked his ass on the field. Monte is a rich entitled prick who couldn't handle a guy on a scholarship with no money and no family being better than him at—well, everything.

Monte is also the ex-boyfriend she was using me to make jealous. The guy she was toying with me to get back. Probably would've worked too if Monte gave a shit about anyone other than himself. But instead of getting jealous and taking her back, he laughed and told me and all the other guys on the team she was sleeping with to be careful. She'd fuck anything in a jersey.

I didn't respond well to finding out the girl I'd been flirting with for weeks, that I was dating, that I was starting to fucking fall for, was a manipulative whore sleeping her way through my teammates in some sick attempt to up her social status. A fact I loudly and drunkenly expressed in front of her and about half the campus at the end of season party. I'll admit slut-shaming her wasn't my finest hour. Okay, it might've been the shittiest thing I've ever done. She has a valid reason to hate me. Like I have one to hate her.

Looks like the tables have turned with Monte begging for a second chance. Now that he's an expelled pariah, she wants nothing to do with him. That just proves I was right about her.

All Michelle Anders cares about is status and finding herself a meal ticket.

Smoke rising from the pan draws my attention back to my charred grilled cheese. I curse under my breath and chuck my burned lunch in the trash. I let the pan drop in the sink with a loud metallic clang. I've lost my appetite.

"What's wrong, princess? Trouble in paradise?" I can't stop myself from asking.

Even from across the living room I can see Michelle's body stiffen at the sound of my voice.

"Not that it is *any* of your damn business, but it was never a paradise."

I scoff. "Glad trying to keep your shitty relationship was worth using decent people." I sound like I've got sand in my vagina. We both know I'm talking about myself. It's been months and I'm still fucking pissed at her. And myself for believing she gave a fuck.

The midget warrior shoots off the couch and faces me full on. "You jocks are all the same. So full of

86

yourself. You can't even comprehend someone not wanting you. I didn't try to hold on to shit. I tossed that asshole away with both hands."

I step around the kitchen island and face her. "Sure, you tossed him... right after he got caught. After he couldn't provide you the future you think you're entitled to."

She steps around the couch and there's nothing between us but empty space, deep resentment and unsated desires.

She furrows her brow and purses her lips. "You don't know what you're talking about. You don't know me at all."

"Oh, I know you. You jersey chasers are all the same, happy to be any asshole's baby mama if they've got enough money or connections."

She blanches, and if I didn't know she was heartless, I'd swear her eyes were filling with tears.

"Fuck you." She storms back toward the hallway. Whipping around just inside the archway. "For your information, smartass, I dumped King of the Douchebags *long* before his fall from grace. I knew he was an asshole back when the rest of you were still giving him fist bumps for hooking up with chicks behind my back. I have no interest in being his — or anyone else's — *baby mama*. And *you* are the only guy I've been with since, you asshole." Her voice cracks and she flinches. She didn't mean to confess that. Her eyes stab into me, lust and fury making them sparkle. "And I don't give a shit if you believe me or not." Angry rant complete, she's gone in a flash and I'm left dumbstruck.

I pull out my phone, my hand shaking, and FaceTime Austin.

"Hey dude. What's up?" His cheery smile pops up on my screen.

"I need to talk to Elizabeth."

"Say what?"

"Your girlfriend, Jacobs. I need to talk to her. Now." My voice is full of building panic.

"Watch your tone, Wright," he warns.

I let out a sigh, my eyes darting to the now empty hallway. "Sorry, man. It's important."

"Fine. Be nice or you'll regret it."

"Hello?" Elizabeth's sweet voice fills my ear.

I'm not sure how to ask this, so I go with brutally blunt. "Has Michelle fucked anyone since Monte dumped her?"

Her jaw drops and she lets out a soft gasp before she stammers, "How could you...that's not... she's not...why would she..."

The camera spins in a shaky blur before Austin's pissed face comes into view. "What the hell did you just say to my girlfriend? She's bright fucking red, man. What did I fu—"

"I asked if Michelle's fucked anyone since Monte dumped her."

"You're such an asshole," Austin says on a disappointed grumble.

"So I've been told. It's important, Austin. I need to know."

"Seriously?" he asks.

"As the grave, man."

He sighs. "Fuck. Fine. Hold on."

The screen fills with what looks like a blank ceiling and I can only hear muffled voices.

"Okay. Let me just say, this is some fucking junior high-level does-she-like-me bullshit," Austin says with an exasperated but amused lilt. "Elizabeth says, first of all, Michelle dumped Monte. Because he is, and I quote, 'a lying, cheating, no-good scoundrel'."

"Fine, whatever. And the other guys?"

"There are no other guys. Just you and Monte."

I keel forward and let out a deep, guttural breath like someone just socked me in the stomach. That's what this feels like. Like someone just knocked me on my ass. *What the fuck did I do?*

"Is she sure?" I ask, my voice weak and shaky.

"Yeah, she's sure. Michelle isn't that kind of girl, man."

"Monte told me... never mind."

Austin's voice gets hard. "Monte is a lying piece of shit. Trust that."

"I know. I know. But I saw Michelle with one of the guys on the team. After we'd already started hanging."

"Saw her doing what?" Austin asks.

I picture walking into the party after Monte warned me Michelle was sleeping around, to find her flirting with one of my teammates. She was smiling and they were leaning into each other. Her hand was on his arm and her tongue was practically in his ear.

"She disappeared on me the first night we met and she was all over Sanchez at the end-of-season party." My voice is ice cold.

Austin laughs at me. "Sanchez is gay, you dumb fuck."

I might throw up. I'm for sure going to punch myself in the face.

Chapter Seventeen

Michelle

I've never been so angry in my life. I hate Andrew Wright with every ounce of my being. To accuse me of sleeping around? Of shopping for a husband? He's got to be kidding me. *How dare he!*

Tears tumble down my cheeks as I toss everything back into my suitcase in a blind fury for the second time in three days. I don't care if I end up sleeping in the woods tonight. I can't spend one more second under the same roof as him.

He's on the phone when I charge out of my bedroom. I don't bother looking at him. I storm over to the fireplace and snatch up the ax that's been there since our first stupid night together. My face flushes with embarrassment when I remember how I threw myself at him. Of course he thinks I'm that kind of girl. I let him take advantage, didn't I? Why wouldn't he think I let every other boy out there have a go too?

Bile rises up the back of my throat and my fingers tighten around the ax handle. I'm not that kind of person. I don't care what he thinks. I know who I am. I know what I'm worth and he can go straight to hell.

"I've gotta go." Drew's voice rings in my ears. He's not talking to me, but the tension in his words catches me off guard. I don't let it deter me. I need to get out of here. *Now.*

Drew reaches the front door before I do and blocks my way. I stare at his chest, picturing his shriveled, rotten heart beneath those muscles.

"We need to talk," he says, his words as soft as when he held me after my night terror.

"Get out of my way," I warn him.

"Please, Michelle."

It's the first time he's said my name and it's a dagger to my heart. I hate that I still want him to be the man to hold me and keep me safe. But he's not. He's a wolf in sheep's clothing.

"Move, Andrew, or so help me." I lift the ax, not even sure myself what I might do. This man has pushed me to my wits' end. "Please," I whimper, hating the weakness in my voice.

He holds up his hands and steps aside.

My heart is racing and my hands shaking when I throw my suitcase into the trunk of my Mini. I toss the ax in next to it and refuse to look up at Drew, who I can feel watching me from the porch. I start the engine and tear out of the driveway.

After a few days of sun, the mud has mostly dried up and the road is drivable if still a little perilous. The danger is worth it for my freedom and sanity. My face is burning hot and tears are just starting to ebb when I pull up to the tree blocking the road. I hear Drew's truck behind me, rumbling up the road. He's following me and that makes me desperate to get away.

I grab the ax again and begin chopping away at the tree with everything I have. I picture Drew's face and my own stupidity. I hack away the desire I have for him. Cut off the memory of his hands on my skin. Sever the toxic hold he has on me. My heart pounds in my ears, my lungs burn and my hands ache, but I keep chopping away at this stupid tree, barely making a dent.

"Michelle," Drew calls from behind me. I don't remember hearing his truck stop or him walk up behind me. I've been lost in a trance.

"Leave me alone," I shout mid-swing, not slowing my frantic pace.

"Michelle, this is a waste of time. You'll need a chainsaw to get through that thing. And you're going to hurt yourself." I know he's right, but I don't care. This is all I have, all I can do to get away.

He takes a step forward, and I nearly clip him with the ax. I'm not aiming for him, but I wouldn't care if I cut into him either.

"What do you care?" I ask, not bothering to look at him. "Just leave me the hell alone!"

"Fine," he says, defeated. He steps away, but I don't hear the truck drive off. He's just standing behind me. Watching me. Waiting.

One final swing and pain shoots up my wrist. I cry out and crumple to the ground. The tears are back, streaming down my cheeks, and I hate myself for being so weak.

Drew is on me in a flash, his deft fingers searching me for an injury. I'm too exhausted to push him away. Too defeated to care. He reaches for the wrist I have cradled in my lap and I wince. My eyes slam shut from the stab of pain.

Suddenly, I'm weightless. He's carrying me and I'm too broken to be indignant.

"God damn it." Rage slurs his words. "I should've stopped you. Tackled you if I had to. Stupid, Andrew. So damn stupid," he mutters admonishments. *To himself?* "You're such an asshole."

I look up into his face. The deep regret carving wrinkles into his forehead confuses the hell out of me. Drew's cradling me against his chest, holding me close. It makes my heart ache worse than my throbbing wrist. My body is shaking and he squeezes me tight.

He carries me to the truck and eases me into the passenger seat before leaning over and buckling me in. He pauses for a moment, dropping his forehead to mine. His breath is warm against my lips when he whispers a pained "I'm so sorry."

He pulls back and is around the truck in a flash. He drives us home in silence.

When we make it to the lake house, Drew sweeps me up in his arms again and carries me to the couch. I'm limp in his hold, my limbs flopping like dead weights when he sets me down. Like a wounded animal caught in a trap, I sit awaiting my fate.

Drew disappears for a moment before returning with pills, water and ice. He hands me two white pills. "Take these. For the swelling. And the pain."

I take them without question, swallowing them down with the water he hands me next.

"Where does it hurt?" he asks. I don't answer. He gently probes my wrist, watching my face for signs he's hurting me. When I don't show any, he says, "I don't think it's broken. But you probably sprained it pretty bad. This should help."

He wraps an ice pack in a hand towel and holds it to my wrist. He lets out a long sigh. He's staring at my forearm, rubbing the inside of it.

"I'm so sorry," he whispers again.

I don't answer, but I watch him with a blank expression. He didn't cause me to hurt my wrist. If anything, he tried to stop me. But I have a feeling he's apologizing for something more.

"I've been such an idiot. And an asshole." He leans forward and places a soft kiss to the palm of my hand before standing up. He paces in front of me, dragging his hands through his hair. I watch the tortured expression on his face, refusing to let hope bubble up inside me.

"You must hate me." He lets out a dry chuckle, a sad and broken sound. "Of course you hate me. *I* hate me. The things I've said about you. To you." His fists ball up at his sides and his face scrunches up like he's in physical pain. "Fuck!" he bellows. The violence and regret in the sound make me gasp. He takes a deep breath and turns to face me. His eyes lock on mine and they're brimming with remorse.

He crosses the room and sits down in front of me on the coffee table. He leans forward, his elbows on his knees, pressing into my personal space.

"I'm going to tell you something. I just need you to let me get it off my chest, then I promise I'll never talk to you again if that's what you want." He waits, watching me like he's waiting for permission. My eyebrows pinch together in confusion, but I nod so he'll continue.

"The first night we met, the party at the football house. You remember?" He pauses again and I nod, refusing to speak to him. "I thought you were amazing. We talked for hours and kissed until I couldn't see straight." A smile ghosts across his lips at the memory. It fades quickly when he continues. "Then you let one of your sorority sisters drag you away and I didn't see you again for the rest of the night."

I remember that night. Kimmie had just broken up with her high school sweetheart and begged me to do shots with her. The next thing I remember was waking up in my bed with the worst hangover of my life. Jessie, our other sorority sister, said she sent us both home early with a designated driver and a bottle of water. Drew must've thought I ditched him to hook up with someone else instead.

I scowl at him, shaking my head. Getting ditched isn't an excuse for being an asshole.

"It's not an excuse, I know," he answers. I tilt my head to the side, wondering for a second if I said that out loud. "I'm just trying to explain why I believed him."

"Who?" I can't help myself from asking.

Drew swallows hard. "Monte. He told me you guys hooked up that night. He told me and a couple of the other guys on the team to watch out. That you slept around. That you were a social climber."

A gasp slips through my lips. I grind my teeth and blow out an angry breath through my nose.

"I know. I know. I didn't want to believe him at first. Then I saw you in the kitchen that night with Sanchez. We'd gone out a couple times. I was really into you." His voice trails off and he wipes his hands on his pants like his palms are sweating. "Anyway, I walked into that party and you were leaning against him, whispering into his ear. He'd just registered for the draft, like me. It all fit."

"Miguel is gay."

"I know that. Now," Drew sheepishly confesses.

"And even if he wasn't, he's a friend of mine," I tell him, my voice getting stronger as the anger builds back up in me. "You think just because I touch a guy, that I'm laughing with him, that I must be sleeping with him?"

"No. But I saw how you were with him and it..." He pinches his eyes shut and grips a handful of his shaggy hair. "It hurt, all right? It fucking hurt to think you didn't care about me. I thought we were...*something*. Together. I thought if we were, you wouldn't...I don't know." He lets out a defeated sigh. "At the time, everything just seemed to make sense."

"Make sense? That I was a slut?" I shoot off the couch and tower over him.

He leans back and holds up his arms in surrender. "No. That you were only interested in guys who could take care of you."

"So, instead of talking to me, the girl you were *really into*, the one you thought you were *something* to—you were, by the way. I was falling in love with you, *asshole*." He sucks in a hard breath at the declaration, but I'm not done. "You decided to announce to half the campus that I was, let me try and remember. What was it?" I think back to that night, my heart breaking at the memory. To hearing him shout across the room to Sanchez about me for half the campus to hear. "Oh, right. *'Wrap it up. That one's a nasty jersey chaser. Wouldn't want to catch anything.'*"

Drew winces. Good. I hope the memory of how horrible he was to me tortures him. I hope it turns his stomach and keeps him up at night.

"You *humiliated* me."

He shakes his head, his eyes watery. "I'm so fucking sorry. I was so damn stupid."

"You can shove your apology up your ass, Wright." He looks smaller somehow, weaker as I stare down at him. "Sorry doesn't change everyone I know thinking I sleep around. Doesn't change that I was too embarrassed to walk around campus those last few months. Doesn't change that everyone was whispering about me, making up stories about how *nasty* I am."

"I know. I hate myself. If there is anything I could do to fix it, I would." He seems earnest, but I don't believe him. I can't afford to.

"It's so easy to sit here now and say sorry. You want to fix it? You want to make it up to me? How about you go back in time and apologize in front of everyone at that party? Why don't you stand up like a man and shout to the world that you are a pathetic, petty, jealous prick who's too blinded by your own ego to see the truth? That you are selfish and small and don't care who you hurt?"

I turn and walk to the edge of the couch. He snatches my good wrist and pleads, "I do care. I was falling in love with you too."

"That's too bad. Because you ruined it." I pull my wrist out of his grip, telling myself I don't care that he looks shattered. That this mountain of a man looks like a single stroke would topple him like so much ash.

I cross the room to the hallway. Without turning around, I tell him over my shoulder, "The only decent thing you can do for me is leave. I don't care where you go, but I can't spend another night under the same roof as you."

I close my bedroom door, lock it and drop to the floor. I cry into the towel he wrapped around my wrist to muffle the sound.

Chapter Eighteen

Drew

I stare up at the beautiful star-filled sky and worry about Michelle for the millionth hour. Instead of hating her, which I never should've done in the first place, I hate myself with a burning passion. I've been kicking my own ass since I got off the phone with Austin, double since she confessed she was falling for me. *She was falling for me.* And I ruined it. I lost her before we ever had a chance.

"Fuck," I curse up to the blackness.

I rack my brain for what else I can try. How I can fix it. I hiked six miles down the road to get her car. I put her bag outside her door before grabbing a bunch of blankets and setting up camp in the back of my truck. She asked me not to stay in the house, and that's the least I can give her.

I call Samantha, needing the ass-chewing only an older sister can deliver.

It's late, but she answers anyway with a knowing, "What's wrong, baby brother?"

I let out a deep sigh. "I've fucked up. I hurt someone I really care about. I didn't mean to. Or, at least, shit. I didn't realize how bad it was until it was too late."

"Hmmm," Sammie muses. "Is this someone a woman?"

"Yes."

"Mm-hmm. Is this the same woman you've been shacking up with all week?"

"We're not *shacking up*," I correct her. Except we kind of are. We had sex. We slept together. My arm reaches out to the side, grasping for the sexy woman who's out of reach. Probably forever. "We're sort of trapped together. She hates me. For good reason."

"Did you apologize?" Sammie asks, like I bumped into someone instead of breaking her heart.

"Yeah, too little too late." I bang my head against the bed of my truck, a metallic thud ringing in my ears.

"Do you care about her?"

I close my eyes and picture Michelle. She's beautiful. There is something about her that I can't seem to shake. "Yes."

"Then fix it." Sammie has always been a pragmatist.

"I tried. I apologized."

"Oh, la-ti-da," my oldest sister teases. "What did you do to her?"

"I humiliated her. And I broke her trust."

"Okay, then fix it."

I'm starting to get annoyed now. "Sammie, I tried."

"Keep trying, idiot," she snips. "You can be such a stubborn ass. Finally put that shit to good use."

"I could say sorry until I'm blue in the face and it's not going to make a difference. She hates me," I say, defeated.

"Listen, women are genetically programmed to forgive. It's a biological imperative that we love you stupid jackasses even when you don't deserve it."

"That's the pregnancy hormones talking. You still haven't forgiven me for throwing up on you at the county fair."

"That *was* my favorite dress." She sighs wistfully.

"I was five. You fed me cotton candy and hot dogs then sent me on the teacups for an hour. You had it coming. And you just proved my point."

"I forgave you when you bought me that purple dress for Christmas."

I groan. "That was like eight years later."

"Yeah, like I said. It might take a while. You said you humiliated her? Then humiliate yourself. Show her you'll humble yourself for her. You said you broke her trust? Rebuild it. Find a way to show her you *really* mean it when you say you're sorry. That they're not empty words. Keep at it, and she'll come around eventually. Probably."

I nod at Sammie's simple wisdom even though she can't see it. "And if none of that works?" I risk asking.

"I don't know, baby brother. Maybe buy her a purple dress?"

We share a small laugh.

"I love you, Sammie."

"Love you too."

I hang up and stare up at the stars again, Sammie's advice rattling around in my brain. *Humble yourself. Show her you mean it.*

There's one thing I could try. It's going to be humiliating as fuck and probably won't make a difference, but it's a start, at least.

Chapter Nineteen

Michelle

I don't remember crawling into bed last night, but I must've at some point because that's where I am when the obnoxious sound of my phone chiming wakes me up. I don't remember setting an alarm, but that constant pinging disagrees. I mash a bunch of buttons with my eyes still closed and am almost back asleep when the damn thing goes off again.

I snatch it up and stare down at it. I've got *thousands* of missed notifications. My jaw drops and I rub my eyes. I must still be asleep. *What the hell is going on?* My phone lights up with an incoming FaceTime.

"You're on SportsCenter!" Jessie shouts in my ear.

I pull the phone away with an annoyed sleep-deprived groan. "What?" I ask.

My bubbly blonde friend is giddy when she repeats, "You're on SportsCenter. Right now. They're talking about you."

I'm too tired for this ridiculousness. "Are you drunk?"

Jessie sighs. "No. I swear. Turn on channel fifty-two. They're talking about you and Andrew Wright. What'd ya do to that boy?"

My throat seizes up and my heart drops to my feet. "Nothing!" I screech. *I didn't murder him in some crazy fever dream, did I?*

"There's a bunch of articles about it too. You're internet famous, babe." My phone pings and I open the link to the article Jessie sent me. The title reads, *'Jackass' Rookie Makes Rookie Mistake.* Sure enough, there's my name along with my Instagram handle. I'm so shocked, I drop my phone.

"I've gotta let you go," I mumble to Jessie, not waiting for a response before I hang up.

I read and re-read the article half a dozen times before I can make any sense out of it. The whole time my phone pings with more and more notifications. Sometime last night, Drew posted something online, some sort of apology, that's got everyone on the internet buzzing about the two of us.

I open my Instagram account and the image of Drew fills my screen. It's dark, but I can make out the stone columns of the lake house in the background. He's flooded with a harsh light, like he's part of some criminal line-up that makes him look guilty as hell. I'm guessing it's the headlights of his truck, since it was definitely taken outside after dark. Like the article claimed, the word *JACKASS* is scribbled across Drew's forehead in big black letters. I can't help but laugh at the sight. Then I look down at Drew's face and my smile fades. His eyebrows are furrowed. His soft lips are turned down into a pitiful pout. His warm brown eyes are overflowing with regret. It's the image of a penitent man. I stare at him, my heart aching. Then I read his caption.

Attention world!!! Time to set the record straight. @MichelleAnders is an amazing, fierce, smart, sweet, loyal and honest woman. And I'm a complete jackass. A pathetic, petty, jealous prick who's been too blinded by my own ego to see the truth – I'm in love with a girl that's too good for me. Rumors are chickenshit and so am I for spreading them. No woman should ever be shamed for what she does – or doesn't – do with her own body. I know better and so should all of you. But I'm selfish and small and I hurt her. And for that I am truly, truly sorry.

I clutch the phone to my chest and laugh until tears roll down my cheeks. The idiot did it. *He actually did it!* He stood up and shouted to the world – digitally, anyway – that he was wrong. I scroll through the thousands of comments. There are plenty giving Drew shit for being 'pussy whipped' and a bunch that detail 'how much ass' he's going to get in the NFL. The idea makes me gag. Many are urging for me to forgive him, after he pays in diamonds. The thought makes me cringe. I'm surprised how many comments are praising me for putting the jerk in his place.

#JackassApology and #SetTheRecordStraight are trending with thousands of people sharing their stories. The women describing being insulted and degraded, disrespected and ditched, break my heart. Men and women pouring their hearts out in apology starts to rebuild my faith in humanity. Drew did this. He started a social media movement to end slut-shaming. For me.

I'm overcome with the need to see those sad brown puppy-dog eyes for myself. I throw open the door to my bedroom and trip over my suitcase. Drew must've brought it in for me last night. I shake my head. He really is a sweet, stupid man. I call his name, but an echo is my only answer. My heart drops when I step into the living room and find it empty.

I shoot down the hallway and toss open the door to the bedroom he was using. His things are gone, but he can't be far. That tree is still down across the road. He has to be here somewhere. The thought fills me with a new sliver of hope.

Without bothering to shower or change or even brush my hair, I barrel out the front of the house. I stop dead in my tracks at the sight of Drew's truck still parked in the driveway. The fist gripping my chest loosens and I draw a full breath.

"Andrew Wright!" I shout at the top of my lungs. Loud enough—if he's within a two-mile radius he'll hear me and hopefully come running.

"Present!" he shouts back, sitting up in the bed of his truck.

My hands fly up and I yelp at the sight, unprepared for him to be so close. I'm struck dumb, watching his massive frame climb out of that truck and turn to face me. He looks disheveled, scruff covering his rugged face, hair a mess, clothes wrinkled and shoulders hunched forward. When my gaze reaches his face, I giggle before slapping my hand over my mouth to keep the sound in. JACKASS is still scribbled across his forehead.

He runs his fingers through his hair, shoves his hands into his pockets and stares down at the ground. He looks like a little kid that got put on time out. He's too adorable for words. My heart swells and this time I don't try to stop it. This time I let myself fall a little bit in love with Andrew Wright.

"Did you sleep in your truck?" I ask him. I'm not sure why I bothered—he clearly did. He nods. "Why?"

"You said you didn't want me under the same roof."

I shake my head and laugh. "So you slept in your truck?"

"Didn't really sleep," he confesses and my heart pinches.

I want to forgive him. I want to trust him. I'm just still not quite sure I can. I promised myself I was done with love. That I was going to be happy. I deserve it. I step off the porch, making my way to him against my better judgment.

"We were on SportsCenter," I tell him. He nods like it's not a big deal. "Because of your post."

"Yeah," he answers, nonplussed.

"It went viral," I prod, waiting for it to register for him. Waiting for the shock and the panic.

He just shrugs. "I'm a first round draft pick about to start his rookie season. I figured it would." He's making a career in professional sports. He has an image to maintain and I don't think *JACKASS* is what his publicist was going for. *Doesn't he care at all?*

"You knew it would get this much attention and you did it anyway? Why?" Waiting for his answer, I hold my breath and hate myself a little bit for it.

"That was kinda the whole point. Shouting it to the world…" His voice trails off and he sighs like someone parked a cement truck on his chest. He walks up to the porch and hits me with that same tortured look he had in the photo. It's even more heartbreaking in person. The last of my resistance crumbles away.

"I'm so fucking sorry." Regret pours out of him.

I cross my arms and steel my features. "I don't forgive you," I tell him. I swear, the big brute's bottom lip actually begins to quiver. "Yet."

Drew's eyes light up and he smiles wide. He cocks an eyebrow and tentatively asks, "Yet?"

"You've got a lot of groveling ahead of you, brute." I let a wicked smile tickle my lips. "We're talking *months* here. Maybe even *years*—"

Drew charges up the porch stairs and silences my threats with a kiss that takes my breath away. He wraps me in his massive arms and my heart dances. Holding me against his hard body, he kisses me with months of regret, days of longing and hours of desire. He kisses me like I'm precious and protected. *Like he loves me.*

Chapter Twenty

Michelle

Try as I might, I can't seem to focus on the steamy romance in my hands. Watching a completely naked Drew saunter out of the crystal-blue lake is so much hotter. The summer sun is beating down on me but watching his manhood swing in the breeze is what's really making my skin burn. *Shrinkage is not a problem for my brute of a man.*

Drew runs his hand through his long shaggy hair and down those chiseled abs, water running off his body in glistening rivulets. I bite my lip and drink in the sight of him. I commit the image to memory, knowing better than to risk taking a picture. *No leaked celebrity nudes for this girl.* I'm still trying to accept that's what Drew is. A celebrity. In a few months, he'll be playing in a stadium full of fans with millions more watching at home. *And he'll be thousands of miles away.* I push the errant thought aside, willing myself to enjoy these moments with him while I have them. I could probably get a hundred thousand dollars for this luscious full frontal from a sleazy tabloid. *Joke's on them.* This view is *priceless.*

"Good book?" he asks with a cocky smirk. He caught me checking him out, something I can't seem to keep myself from indulging in, but I've stopped bothering to hide it. He takes a moment to admire me in nothing but my sunhat and a smile. The hunger in his eyes has made skinny dipping at the lake house my new favorite summer pastime.

"Good *man.*" I beckon him with a quirk of my finger.

He flops down on top of me in a flash, bracing himself on his elbows to keep from crushing me before slowly lowering his cool body onto mine. My nipples peak at the chilly brush of his chest.

"You summoned me, princess," he murmurs in my ear before kissing a wet trail down my neck to my eagerly awaiting breasts.

I hum in appreciation for the teasing touch. I wrap my legs around him, pulling his hips flush against my core and rocking into him.

He has pampered me these past few days, giving in to my every whim or desire. Like midday skinny dipping. I'm not sure I ever want his apologizing to stop. But it will. Soon. *When he's two thousand miles away.* My body stiffens and I pinch my eyes shut. I count to ten in my head.

"What's up?" Drew asks, pulling back with a look of concern chiseled into his furrowed brow. I swear, this man can read my body like a book. I might as well hire a skywriter to spell out my insecurities in the clear blue expanse above us.

"Nothing." I lean forward to kiss him, but he shifts away.

"I call bullshit." Drew unlatches my hands from around his neck and pins my wrists above my head. If it's supposed to be a punishment, he's dead wrong. Naked Drew Wright pinning me down and having his way with me is my all-time favorite fantasy. "You're stiff as a board."

"And you're hard as a rock." My voice drips with seduction. And I'm right, he is hard. *For me.*

"And I'd love to fuck you. Right here. Where anyone could see." The thought sends a thrill down my spine. Apparently, I'm a bit of an exhibitionist. Keeping my hands pinned, he takes my hard nipple in his mouth and bites down with firm pressure. Not hard enough to hurt, but enough to make me shiver. Desire pools between my thighs. "But first you have to tell me what's wrong."

"Nothing's wrong." My voice cracks.

"Liar." He grinds his length against my throbbing clit, torturing me with long, hard strokes before pulling away and leaving me desperate.

"Fuck me." I meant that to come out as a demand, but it's a plea.

"Tell me and I will, princess." He bites my nipple again, grinding against me and drawing primal sounds out of me that no woman has ever made. I cave to the sweet torment.

"I'm just sad this is ending."

"Ending?" His voice gets hard and his hold on my wrists tightens. "*What* is ending?"

"This. *Us.*"

"The fuck it is." He claims my mouth with a punishing kiss. His body presses into mine, enveloping me in his angry lust. Against my lips he growls, "Get it through that hard head of yours. You're mine, Michelle."

My name on his lips and his hard cock gliding over my slit in the perfect rough rhythm send me over the edge. I come apart underneath him, writhing in pleasure. I catch my breath as he plants delicate kisses on my collarbone and chest. His tenderness shatters me. I blink back the tears and will my lip to stop quivering.

"Why do you think this would end?" His voice is a soft purr in my ear. "I've got years of *groveling* to do."

"That you're going to do from thousands of miles away? You're heading off to Wisconsin to be some NFL superstar and I'm moving back in with my parents in California and hunting for any writing job I can get my hands on." The confession tumbles out of me. I try to tug my wrists out of his grasp. To pull away. *Run away.* But Drew's steadfast grip doesn't waver. His eyes burn into me.

"Come with me."

"What?"

"Come with me," he says again. Not a request. A command.

"No." I try again to free myself. And again, I fail.

"Why not?"

"Because I'm not a succubus looking for a meal ticket. I'm pretty sure we've been over this," I bite out. My insecurities are getting the better of me.

"Fine. Then we'll split everything fifty-fifty. Rent. Groceries. Utilities. Fuck, I'll even let you chip in for gas money. Whatever you want. I'm not offering you a meal ticket." He interlaces his fingers with mine and locks his serious gaze on me. "Just my heart." He drops his forehead to mine and whispers, "Come with me. Please. I love you."

My heart breaks open and tears stream down my face.

"I love you too," I blurt out.

The past few days have been a whirlwind. Ups and downs. Soaring in the heavens and wallowing in the mud. But this moment? This might be the best moment of my life.

"Is that a yes? You'll come with me?" Drew asks with cautious excitement.

"Yes." I smile at the joy lighting up his face like one of those stadiums he'll be playing in soon.

Drew releases my hands and I pull him in for a deep and demanding kiss. I slide my hand between us, guiding him to my entrance. Only one thing will make this moment better — having Drew inside me. Nothing between us. Just him and me, raw and honest. I shift to seat the tip of his cock inside me and he groans, a low and guttural sound that makes me even wetter.

"Make love to me, Drew." I swear, he gets harder at the sound of his name falling from my lips.

"Yes, ma'am."

He enters me in slow, steady thrusts. The wind whips around us and the sun beats down as Andrew Wright makes sweet love to me. I've never felt anything like the connection we have. We move together. Breathe together. Our hearts beat together.

"I love you, Drew," I tell him again.

"I love you," he echoes.

His pace quickens and I'm tumbling toward the edge of an abyss. His hard length stretching me, filling me completely, pushes me to the brink of insanity. I'm crazy for this man.

"I'm close," I confess with a panting breath.

"Come for me, princess. Come for me, Michelle." And I do, hard and long, my toes curling with divine pleasure and every muscle in my body burning with ecstasy. My inner walls tense around him, sending him over the edge of his own climax, a feral roar torn from him.

Adrenaline and endorphins flood my body, but it's the feel of Drew's lips on mine when he finds his release that make my heart flutter. His kisses are a gentle promise, a plea to keep his heart safe. Because it belongs to me now.

And mine belongs to him.

I thought I hated Andrew Wright. I thought I was done with love. Turns out I was wrong. This doesn't just feel right. It feels *perfect*.

Epilogue

Three Years Later
Drew

Firelight dances across Michelle's delicate face and my breath catches. She is beautiful. Mostly submerged in the giant tub, soap sliding down her collarbone into the hint of her chest under the thick bubbles is enough to have me desperate to be inside her. My girlfriend. My best friend. Hopefully, soon, my wife.

I take my time, enjoying watching her run those slender fingers down her toned legs. That silky black hair I love to feel gripped in my fist is pinned up, with only a few loose stands clinging to her damp skin. If I weren't already hopelessly in love with this woman, the sight of her naked in that tub would seal the deal.

"You coming, brute? Or just going to ogle me all night?" the love of my life taunts.

She trails that soft gaze up my body, pausing at my hard cock while her lips tick up into a smirk. When her eyes find mine, she tilts her chin down and hitches her eyebrow up in an inquisitive challenge.

"Believe me, princess. Coming is definitely on the agenda tonight. For both of us."

She crooks a finger and beckons me to her. Leaning forward, she makes room for my huge body behind her. I've never been small, but three years in the NFL and I'm a beast. The warm water relaxes my overworked muscles as I ease into it. Michelle settles back between my thighs, her head resting against my chest.

She closes her eyes and hums. "I love the off-season."

I kiss her temple, wrap my arms around her and pull her close. "So do I. But not as much as I love you."

Her body shakes with laughter. "You're such a cornball." She stretches up and kisses my neck. She nuzzles into me in the way that melts my insides. "And I love it. But not as much as I love *you*," she whispers.

I let out a low chuckle.

I grab a loofa off the edge of the tub, dunk it in the warm water and run light touches over her chest and arms.

"How long can we stay?" I ask. I may be built like a brick house, a beast on the field — defensive player of the year two years running — and make a shit ton of money, but this woman is the boss. She runs our life and I wouldn't have it any other way.

"Two weeks. Then we're at Sammie's for a week."

I let out a low groan. I love our time at the lake house, but it never seems to be long enough. I've been hounding Elizabeth for three years to sell it to me, but no luck yet. At least she lets us come up here every year. Our life is crazy busy, but the time we can steal away from it all, out here where it's just me and Michelle's amazing body, is what keeps me sane.

"Hush. They're your family."

"And?" I mentally debate hiring a guy to come cut a tree down to block the road.

She shakes her head against me. "And they love you. And we love them. So, put on your big boy pants and enjoy it."

"Easy for you to say. You're not the lone dude surrounded by enough estrogen to fill the Grand Canyon."

Michelle's laugh has her ass sliding against my dick and I moan, even though we're arguing about my family.

"Sammie's husband will be there." Michelle is determined to keep arguing, despite the fact that her voice is breathy and her hips are circling over mine.

I pull her down onto me and nip at her neck. "Darren isn't a dude. Sammie has bigger balls than that guy."

Desire is building in Michelle—I can feel it in her tensing body. "You got a problem with strong women, brute?"

A grin twists up my lips. "Not at all. I love fucking a strong woman."

Michelle shoots up and spins around. "You're such an ass," she says on a mock gasp. I reach for her, but she tsks and pulls away.

I lean back and enjoy the sight of her reclining against the far end of the tub. She pretends to ignore me, grabbing the loofa and washing her neck and chest in a luscious tease. I grab each of her ankles and spread her legs. Her eyes go wide and she bites her lip. I trail my hand up her leg and her breath hitches. When I reach her knee, I hit her ticklish spot and she jerks up with a gasp. A deep laugh rumbles out of me.

"Jerk." She play-kicks me.

I hold my hands up in surrender. She narrows her eyes on me, so I pick up her ankle and commence an apology foot rub. It works. Like always.

"What's after Sammie's?" I ask.

"Then it's my folks." Michelle lets out a frustrated sigh.

"What's up? I love your folks."

"Of course you do. You get to hang out with Dad in the den and watch sports. I get to listen to the never-ending guilt trip from my mom about how old she is and how she'll die before she ever gets any grandbabies." Her head hits the back of the tub with a clank.

I slide my hands up the outside of her thighs under the water. When I reach her hips, I pull her forward so she's straddling my lap. She sinks down with a soft moan. I grip her neck and pull her lips to meet mine, claiming them in a searing kiss. She melts for me, not noticing my other hand reaching for the secret I have hidden next to one of the claw feet of the tub.

The cool metal beneath my fingertips, I nip Michelle's lip and ask, "Why don't we give her some then?"

She pulls back, the familiar confused wrinkle settling in her forehead. "Give her what? Grandbabies?"

I nod, unable to keep the naughty smile off my lips. "Think Elizabeth will mind if I knock you up in her family's tub?"

"Knock me up?" Michelle scoffs. "You better marry me first, brute. I refuse to be some jock's baby momma!" She throws her head back and laughs.

I swallow the lump in my throat and hold up the engagement ring between us. "Well, if you insist."

"Oh my gaaaawd!" Michelle screeches, her hands slapping over her mouth and her eyes going as wide as silver dollars. She starts to cry and shake her hands like she does when she's trying to dry her nails. "Are you serious?"

"As the grave, princess." I wrap an arm around her small waist and pull her flush against me. "Michelle Anders, will you make me the luckiest man in the world and marry me?"

She grabs both sides of my face and slams her lips against mine, kissing me frantically.

"Is that a yes?" I ask through squished cheeks.

Michelle throws her arms up in the air, smiles wide and screams, "YES!"

I grab her hand, ignoring how mine is shaking, and slide the diamond onto her ring finger. I kiss her hand with a smile.

"I knew it," I declare.

"Knew what?"

"That you'd be Mrs. Wright."

So Far, So Good:
So Not My Type
Amelia Kingston

Excerpt

"You can get out of my way or you can die. The choice is yours. You've got to the count of ten," I crow into the mic of my headset. *I love this game.* Destroying egotistical douche canoes in Rule Them All is one of my all-time favorite things. And I'm good at it. I was born to dominate this computer world with an iron fist.

"That time of the month, Trix?" The snotty, barely post-pubest voice rings in my ear. He must be new.

Wrong choice, dipshit. A wicked smile twists my red-stained lips.

"One. Two. Ten. Time's up." With a few keystrokes my digital army squashes my enemies with brutal efficiency.

"Holy shit." The woeful cry is music to my ears. "I was just playing around."

"Awww. Poor baby. Next time you feel like *playing* I suggest you stay the fuck away from Woman's-World."

Yes, I named my make-believe country Woman'sWorld. And yes, I have zero remorse in exterminating pests like this one. He can't say I didn't warn him. Rule Them All is not for the timid or insecure. It's a dog-eat-dog world with player-controlled countries clawing at one another to get to the top. To be the best. My gamer handle is DominaTrix for a reason.

"Wow, Jackie, that was harsh," my best friend chastises me in our private video chat. Elizabeth is a bleeding heart. I love her to death, but she wants to think the best of everyone. Truth is, some people are just assholes. A little bit of humbling goes a long way.

"He had it coming," her boyfriend, Austin, chimes in. I nearly cut his balls off last year when he broke Elizabeth's heart. Believe me, *he* had it coming too. I think he's still trying to get on my good side. I promise I have one — it's just reserved for a very select group of truly amazing people. The rest of the world can fuck right off.

"Thanks, Man Meat. But I don't need your approval." I flip off the camera with a sweet smile. He chuckles and Elizabeth groans.

"Isn't it like three in the morning for you?" she asks.

I glance across my small studio apartment to the clock on the milkcrate that serves as my nightstand.

"Shit. Guess tomorrow's going to be a bitch." I shrug, hugging my knee up to my chest and smiling at my best friend through the camera.

She rolls her eyes at me. "Did you at least finish your submission for the contest?"

My gaze darts up to the dozens of half-finished designs taped up on nearly every square inch of wall space.

"Almost," I lie.

"Almost?" She calls me out with the same disappointed tone my mom uses. The sound is like a tiny needle poking me in the eye.

"Yeah, almost. As in just about. Nearly."

"As in no."

"I'll finish it tomorrow." It's a bold-faced lie and we both know it.

Every year, E.B. Jericho, one of my all-time favorite sci-fi writers, holds a contest to design the cover art for her latest release. And every year I promise myself I'll enter. I come up with a million and one ideas, but I always let the deadline for submission pass me by. I've been torturing myself for months trying to come up with a unique idea, but nothing seems right.

"You better. You've got this thing on lockdown." Elizabeth's faith in me is unwavering, despite the fact that I've never actually had any paid graphic artist work. "You've read every one of his books, what? Like a dozen times?"

"*Her* books and at least a dozen."

No one really knows who E.B. Jericho is. She's a notorious recluse, but Elizabeth and I have a standing bet on the author's gender. She goes with odds, seeing as how seventy-five percent of sci-fi writers are men. I am convinced E.B. is a woman. She's too clever and witty not to be. If we ever met, we'd be hetro-lifemates. Instant besties for sure.

"Alright, kiddos. I better get my beauty sleep." I blow a kiss at the screen.

"Night, Jackie," Austin's deep voice announces.

"Night. Love you, babe," Elizabeth chirps with a sweet smile.

"Love you too."

I click off the camera, toss my glasses onto my desk and shut down my computer. Stretching my arms up and taking a long, deep breath, I sweep my gaze over the design ideas splattering my walls again. *None of them is good enough.* It's so late it's early, but my mind is still racing. The idea of having to pick a design and submit it for someone I admire to judge makes me nauseous.

I grab my sketchbook and sprawl out in my tangled mess of an unmade bed. Closing my eyes, I picture Persei Rivera, the main character from E.B. Jericho's *Honorbound*. She's a space smuggler and the most kickass character of all time. She's standing tall in front of her ship, Phobos, a Hellhound-class light space cruiser. Her grease-stained cargo pants are tucked into lunar-dust-speckled boots. Her father's old leather jacket is zipped up to keep out the chill on the darkside of the deserted space rock where she's currently stowing cargo. The wind blows her raven-black hair in thick waves behind her and her pale skin appears nearly translucent. The low light from a distant sun glints off the laser pistol strapped to her hip. Her arms are crossed and the edge of her mouth is quirked up in a devious challenge. She's the Dirty Harry of space. She *wants* you to try something. *Punk*.

In my mind, the sight is clear as day. I spring my eyes open and stare down at the blank page. Two strokes of my pen and it's already gone wrong. I rip the page out of my sketchbook, crumple it into a tiny ball and toss it across the room with a huff. I try again, but I can't get the angle right for Phobos. She's an impressive ship and *I made her look like a bathtub toy*! Another page ripped out. Another discarded failure.

Over and over again, I doodle the same intergalactic scene until my eyelids get heavy and I pass out in a heap of crumpled paper.

* * * *

The obnoxious beeping of my alarm startles me awake. With a loud groan and a quick kick, I send the institutionalized torture device flying across the room. The beeping gets softer, sadder, before finally stopping. I'm the wrong way round in my bed on top of the covers. I pick my head up and the crinkling of paper echoes in my ear. I stare down at my latest creation, the sleek starship smudged and ruined with my drool. *Great.* I swipe the whole mess into a pile on the floor. I'm back asleep before I can regret the half-conscious decision.

Untold hours later, I'm stirred awake again by the less than gentle but very familiar poke of a wooden cane in my side. I push it away and roll over, but the poking persists.

"What?" I whine.

"Oh, so you are alive." The bed dips beside me and I crack my eyes open to stare up at Pops' sly smile. "I was beginning to think it was just the wistful delusion of an old man that I had a brilliant and punctual granddaughter."

I flop onto my back and stretch out my arms and legs, curling my toes with a satisfied moan.

"Brilliant, sure. Punctual, not so much."

Pops hums. "A man can dream. But now it's time for you to face the day. Life goes on whether you're living it or not, my love," he quips, with a final poke in the ribs for good measure.

"Yes, Sir." I give him a two-finger salute and a huge smile. With an achy groan, he stands and strides to the door. "Did you take your pills?" I call to his retreating back.

"Get to work, young lady," he snips playfully.

"Take your pills, old man," I yell back.

Fifteen minutes later I'm downstairs in Pops' coffee shop, unlocking the door and waiting for the morning to be over. I pick up the copy of *Honorbound* I have stashed under the register, lean against the counter and get to reading.

"Excuse me." A snide voice interrupts my search for galactic inspiration. I look up to find a twenty-something Instagram influencer glaring at me. Dressed head-to-toe in skin-tight gym clothes that have never seen a drop of sweat and a sleek ponytail containing her bottle-blonde locks, this valley princess taps her nail extensions on my counter. "I'm ready to order."

"What do you want?" My tone is flat. I set my book down and meet her judgmental gaze.

She scoffs, her displeasure evident in her sour pout and not-so-subtle head shake. "Large non-fat iced latte with three pumps of vanilla, two pumps of caramel and four Splenda."

"Five seventy-five." I rattle off a price, clicking a few buttons on our ancient register.

She hands me a twenty. I hand her back her change, which she takes the time to count with a watchful eye before her lycra-covered ass sashays away. I suppress a gag and make her latte with *full fat* milk and real sugar.

"Latte," I call out.

She takes a sip and I laugh at the sight of her nearly doing a spit take.

"I said non-fat. This is definitely *not* non-fat." The look of disgust on her face makes wish I'd added a little *special sauce*. I mean spit.

"And?"

"And I specifically said *non*-fat." She shakes her head, looking me up and down. "You really should get your act together if you want to be taken seriously."

I bite my tongue, shoving down the urge to tell her to go fuck herself. This is Pops' place after all.

With a hair toss, she's nearly out the door when I shout, "Want my mom's number? You'd get along great!"

I mutter angrily to myself, before picking up my book and trying to put her out of my mind.

Home of Erotic Romance

Sign up for our newsletter and find out about all our romance book releases, eBook sales and promotions, sneak peeks and FREE romance books!

About the Author

Amelia Kingston is many things, the most interesting of which are probably California girl, writer, traveler, and dog mom. She survives on chocolate, coffee, wine, and sarcasm. Not necessarily in that order.

She's been blessed with a patient husband who's embraced her nomad ways and traveled with her to over 30 countries across 5 continents (I'm coming for you next, Antarctica!). She's also been cursed with an impatient (although admittedly adorable) terrier who pouts when her dinner is 5 minutes late.

She writes about strong, stubborn, flawed women and the men who can't help but love them. Her irreverent books aim to be silly and fun with the occasional storm cloud to remind us to appreciate the sunny days. As a hopeless romantic, her favorite stories are the ones that remind us all that while love is rarely perfect, it's always worth chasing.

Amelia loves to hear from readers. You can find her contact information, website details and author profile page at https://www.totallybound.com